How to Teach Religion

George Herbert Betts

Contents

HOW TO TEACH RELIGION

BY

George Herbert Betts

EDITOR'S INTRODUCTION

The teacher of religion needs to be very sure of himself at one point. He ought to be able to answer affirmatively the question, "Have I the prophetic impulse in my teaching?" Sooner or later, practical difficulties will "come not singly but by battalions," and the spirit needs to be fortified against discouragement. When driven back to the second or third line defense it is important that such a line really exists; the consciousness of being the spokesman for God makes the teacher invulnerable and unconquerable.

But in order that this divine impulse may attain its greatest strength and find the most direct, articulate, and effective expression, the teacher must know *how* as well as *what* to teach. The most precious spiritual energy may be lost because improperly directed or controlled. Unhesitating insight into the solution of practical problems helps to open up a channel through which the prophetic impulse can find fullest expression.

There is no substitute for mastery of the technique of the teaching process. Prayerful consecration cannot take its place. This ready command of the methods of teaching, on the other hand, is in no sense an equivalent of the consciousness of having been "called" or "chosen" to teach religion. The two must go hand in hand. No one who feels himself divinely appointed for this sacred task dares ignore the responsibility of becoming a "workman not to be ashamed, *rightly* dividing the word of truth."

This volume by Dr. Betts offers the earnest teacher of religion an exceptional opportunity to make more effective his ideal of instruction. The treatment applies the best of modern educational science to the problems of the church school, without, however, for a moment, forgetting that a vital religious experience is the final goal of all our teaching.

Besides setting forth the underlying principles of religious teaching in a clear and definite way, the author has included in every chapter a rich fund of illustration and concrete application which cannot fail to prove immediately helpful in every church classroom. It is also believed that students of religious education will find this treatment of method by Professor Betts the most fundamental and sane that has yet appeared in the field.

NORMAN E. RICHARDSON.

AUTHOR'S PREFACE

C hildren can be brought to a religious character and experience through right nurture and training in religion. This is the fundamental assumption on which the present volume rests, and it makes the religious education of children the most strategic opportunity and greatest responsibility of the church, standing out above all other obligations whatever.

Further, the successful teaching of religion is based on the same laws that apply to other forms of teaching; hence teachers in church schools need and have a right to all the help that a scientific pedagogy permeated by an evangelistic spirit can give them. They also have the obligation to avail themselves of this help for the meeting of their great task.

This book undertakes to deal in a concrete and practical way with the underlying principles of religious instruction. The plan of the text is simple. First comes the part *the teacher* must play in training the child in religion. Then the spiritual changes and growth to be effected in *the child* are set forth as the chief objective of instruction. Next is a statement of the *great aims,* or goals, to be striven for in the child's expanding religious experience. These goals are: (1) fruitful *religious knowledge*; (2) right *religious attitudes--interests, ideals, feelings, loyalties*; (3) the *application of this knowledge and these attitudes to daily life and conduct*.

Following the discussion of aims is the question of just *what subject matter* to choose in order to accomplish these ends, and *how best to organize* the chosen material for instruction. And finally, *how most effectively to present* the subject matter selected to make it serve its purpose in stimulating and guiding the spiritual growth and development of children.

The volume is intended as a textbook for teacher-training classes, students of religious education, and for private study by church-school teachers. It is also hoped that ministers may find some help in its pages toward meeting their educational problems.

Northwestern University, Evanston, Illinois.

CHAPTER I
THE TEACHER HIMSELF

It is easy enough to secure buildings and classrooms for our schools. The expenditure of so many dollars will bring us the equipment we require. Books and materials may be had almost for the asking. The great problem is to secure *teachers*--real teachers, teachers of power and devotion who are able to leave their impress on young lives. Without such teachers all the rest is but as sounding brass or a tinkling cymbal. And to be a real teacher is a very high achievement.

Bishop Vincent was giving a lecture on "That Boy." He himself was "that boy," and in the course of describing his school days he fell into meditation as follows: "That old school master of mine!--He is dead now--and I have forgiven him!--And I am afraid that was the chronology of the matter; for I never was able to forgive him while he lived." I, as one of the listeners, smiled at the bitter wit of the speaker, but was oppressed.

This somber view of the impression sometimes left by teachers on their pupils received an antidote the following day, however, when a venerable old man approached my desk bearing in his hands an ancient and dog-eared copy of a text in grammar. He opened the book and proudly showed me written across the fly leaf "Grover Cleveland, President." Then he told me this story:

"I have been a teacher. In one of my first schools I had Grover Cleveland as a pupil. He came without a textbook in grammar, and I loaned him mine. Years passed, and Grover Cleveland was President of the United States. One day I was one of many hundreds passing in line at a public reception to grasp the President's hand. I carried this book with me, and when it came my turn to meet the President, I presented the volume and said, 'Mr. President, do you recognize this book, and do you remember me?' In an instant the light of recognition had flashed in Mr. Cleveland's eyes. Calling me by name, he grasped my hand and held it while the crowd waited and while he recalled old times and thanked me for what I had meant to him when I was his teacher. Then he took the old book and autographed it for me."

Three types of teachers.--Two types of teachers are remembered: one to be forgiven after years have softened the antagonisms and resentments; the other to be thought of with honor and gratitude as long as memory lasts. Between these two is a third and a larger group: those who are *forgotten*, because they failed to stamp a lasting impression on their pupils. This group represents the *mediocrity* of the profession, not bad enough to be actively forgiven, not good enough to claim a place in gratitude and remembrance.

To which type would we belong? To which type *can* we belong? Can we choose? What are the factors that go to determine the place we shall occupy in the scale of teachers?

THE PERSONAL FACTOR

When we revert to our own pupil days we find that the impressions which cling to our memories are not chiefly impressions of facts taught and of lessons learned, but of the *personality* of the teacher. We may have forgotten many of the truths presented and most of the conclusions drawn, but the warmth and glow of the human touch still remains.

To be a teacher of religion requires a particularly exalted personality. The teacher and the truth taught should always leave the impression of being of the same pattern. "For their sakes I sanctify myself," said the Great Teacher; shall the teachers of his Word dare do less!

The teacher as an interpreter of truth.--This is not to say that the subject matter taught is unimportant, nor that the lessons presented are immaterial. It is only to say that life responds first of all to *life*. Truth never comes to the child disembodied and detached, but always with the slant and quality of the teacher's interpretation of it. It is as if the teacher's mind and spirit were the stained glass through which the sunlight must fall; all that passes through the medium of a living personality takes its tone and quality from this contact. The pupils may or may not grasp the lessons of their books, but their teachers are living epistles, known and read by them all.

For it is the concrete that grips and molds. Our greatest interest and best attention center in persons. The world is neither formed nor reformed by abstract truths nor by general theories. Whatever ideals we would impress upon others we must first have realized in ourselves. What we **are** often drowns out what we say. Words and maxims may be misunderstood; character seldom is. Precepts may fail to impress; personality never does. God tried through the ages to reveal his purposes to man by means of the law and the prophets, but man refused to heed or understand. It was only when God had made his thought and plan for man concrete in the person of Jesus of Nazareth that man began to understand.

The first and most difficult requirement of the teacher, therefore, is--himself, his personality. He must combine in himself the qualities of life and character he seeks to develop in his pupils. He must look to his personality as the source of his influence and the measure of his power. He must be the living embodiment of what he would lead his pupils to become. He must live the religion he would teach them. He must possess the vital religious experience he would have them attain.

The building of personality.--Personality is not born, it is made. A strong, inspiring personality is not a gift of the gods, nor is a weak and ineffective personality a visitation of Providence. Things do not **happen** in the realm of the spiritual any more than in the realm of nature. Everything is **caused**. Personality grows. It takes its form in the thick of the day's work and its play. It is shaped in the crush and stress of life's problems and its duties. It gains its quality from the character of the thoughts and acts that make up the common round of experience. It bears the marks of whatever spiritual fellowship and communion we keep with the Divine.

Professor Dewey tells us that character is largely dependent on the mode of assembling its parts. A teacher may have a splendid native inheritance, a fine education, and may move in the best social circles, and yet not come to his best in personality. It requires some high and exalted task in order to assemble the powers and organize them to their full efficiency. The urge of a great work is needed to make potential ability actual. Paul did not become the giant of his latter years until he took upon himself the great task of carrying the gospel to the Gentiles.

Our own responsibility.--It follows then that the building of our personalities is largely in our own hands. True, the influence of heredity is not to be overlooked. It is easier for some to develop attractive, compelling qualities than for others. The raw material of our nature comes with us; is what heredity decrees. But the finished product bears the stamp of our training and development. Fate or destiny never takes the reins from our hands. We are free to shape ourselves largely as we will.

Our inner life will daily grow by what it feeds upon. This is the great secret of personality-building. What to-day we build into thought and action to-morrow becomes character and personality. Let us cultivate our interests, think high thoughts, and give ourselves to worthy deeds, and these have soon become a life habit. Let our hearts go out in helpfulness to those about us, and sympathy for human kind becomes a compelling motive in our lives before we are aware. Let us consciously listen to the still small voice speaking to the soul, and we will find our souls expanding to meet the Infinite.

The secret.--He who would develop his personality into the full measure of its strength and power must, then, set his goal at *living constantly in the presence of the* BEST. This will include the best in thought and memory and anticipation. It will permit none but cheerful moods, nor allow us to dwell with bitterness upon petty wrongs and grievances. It will control the tongue, and check the unkind word or needless criticism. It will cause us to seek for the strong and beautiful qualities in our friends and associates, and not allow us to point out their faults nor magnify their failings. It will cure us of small jealousies and suppress all spirit of revenge. It will save us from idle worry and fruitless rebellion against such ills as cannot be cured. In short, it will free our lives from the crippling influence of negative moods and critical attitudes. It will teach us to *be ruled by our admirations rather than by our aversions*.

Above all, he who would build a personality fitted to serve as the teacher of the child in his religion must constantly live in the presence of *the best he can attain in God*. There is no substitute for this. No fullness of intellectual power and grasp, no richness of knowledge gleaned, and no degree of skill in instruction can take the place of a vibrant, immediate, Spirit-filled consciousness of God in the heart. For religion is *life*, and the best definition of religion we can present to the child is the example and warmth of a life inspired and vivified by contact with the Source of all spiritual being. The authority of the teacher should rest on his own religious experience, rather than on the spiritual experience of others.

A character chart.--There is no possibility, of course, of making a list of all the qualities that enter into our personalities. Nor would it be possible to trace all the multiform ways in which these qualities may combine in our characters. It is worth while, however, to consider a few of the outstanding traits which take first place in determining our strength or weakness, and especially such as will respond most readily to conscious training and cultivation. Such a list follows. Each quality may serve as a goal both for our own development and for the training of our pupils.

POSITIVE QUALITIES	NEGATIVE QUALITIES
1 Open-minded, inquiring, broad	Narrow, dogmatic, not hungry for truth
2 Accurate, thorough, discerning	Indefinite, superficial, lazy
3 Judicious, balanced, fair	Prejudiced, led by likes and dislikes
4 Original, independent, resourceful	Dependent, imitative, subservient
5 Decisive, possessing convictions	Uncertain, wavering, undecided
6 Cheerful, joyous, optimistic	Gloomy, morose, pessimistic, bitter
7 Amiable, friendly, agreeable	Repellent, unsociable, disagreeable
8 Democratic, broadly sympathetic	Snobbish, self-centered, exclusive
9 Tolerant, sense of humor, generous	Opinionated, dogmatic, intolerant
10 Kind, courteous, tactful	Cruel, rude, untactful
11 Tractable, cooperative, teachable	Stubborn, not able to work with others
12 Loyal, honorable, dependable	Disloyal, uncertain dependability
13 Executive, forceful, vigorous	Uncertain, weak, not capable
14 High ideals, worthy, exalted	Low standards, base, contemptible
15 Modest, self-effacing	Egotistical, vain, autocratic
16 Courageous, daring, firm	Overcautious, weak, vacillating
17 Honest, truthful, frank, sincere	Low standards of honor and truth
18 Patient, calm, equable	Irritable, excitable, moody
19 Generous, open-hearted, forgiving	Stingy, selfish, resentful
20 Responsive, congenial	Cold, repulsive, uninviting
21 Punctual, on schedule, capable	Tardy, usually behindhand, incapable
22 Methodical, consistent, logical	Haphazard, desultory, inconsistent

23 Altruistic, given to service	Indifferent, not socially-minded
24 Refined, alive to beauty, artistic	Coarse, lacking aesthetic quality
25 Self-controlled, decision, purpose	Suggestible, easily led, uncertain
26 Good physical carriage, dignity	Lack of poise, ill posture, no grace
27 Taste in attire, cleanliness, pride	Careless in dress, frumpy, no pride
28 Face smiling, voice pleasing	Somber expression, voice unpleasant
29 Physical endurance, vigor, strength	Quickly tired, weak, sluggish
30 Spiritual responsiveness strong	Spiritually weak, inconstant, uncertain
31 Prayer life warm, satisfying	Prayer cold, formal, little comfort
32 Religious certainty, peace, quiet	Conflict, strain, uncertainty
33 Religious experience expanding	Spiritual life static or losing force
34 God a near, inspiring reality	God distant, unreal, hard of approach
35 Power to win others to religion	Influence little or negative
36 Interest in Bible and religion	Little concern for religion and Bible
37 Religion makes life fuller and richer	Religion felt as a limitation
38 Deeply believe great fundamentals	Lacking in foundations for faith
39 Increasing triumph over sin	Too frequent falling before temptation
40 Religious future hopeful	Religious growth uncertain

It is highly instructive for one to grade himself on this list of qualities; or he may have his friends and associates grade him, thus getting an estimate of the impression he is making on others. Teachers will find it well worth while to attempt to grade each of their pupils; for this will give a clearer insight into their strengths and weaknesses, and so indicate where to direct our teaching. Mark each separate set of qualities on the scale of 10 for the highest possible attainment. If the strength of the *positive* qualities of a certain set (as in No. 10) can be marked but 6, then the negative qualities of this set must carry a mark of 4.

THE TEACHER'S BACKGROUND OF PREPARATION

One can never teach all he knows. Dr. John Dewey tells us that the subject matter of our instruction should be so well mastered that it has become second nature to us; then when we come to the recitation we can give our best powers of thought and insight to the ***human element***--seeking to understand the boys and girls as we teach them.

Our knowledge and mastery must always be much broader than the material we actually present. It must be deeper and our grasp more complete than can be reached by our pupils. For only this will give us the mental perspective demanded of the teacher. Only this will enable our thought to move with certainty and assurance in the field of our instruction. And only this will win the confidence and respect of our pupils who, though their minds are yet unformed, have nevertheless a quick sense for mastery or weakness as revealed in their teacher.

A danger confronted by teachers in church schools.--Teachers in our church schools are at a disadvantage at this point. They constitute a larger body than those who teach in the day schools, yet the vast army who teach our children religion receive no salaries. They are engaged in other occupations, and freely give their services as teachers of religion with no thought of compensation or reward. The time and enthusiasm they give to the Sunday school is a free-will offering to a cause in which they believe. All this is inspiring and admirable, but it also contains an element of danger.

For it is impossible to set up scholastic and professional standards for our teachers of religion as we do for the teachers in our day schools. The day-school teacher, employed by the state and receiving public funds, must go through a certain period of training for his position. He must pass examinations in the subject matter he is to teach, and in his professional fitness for the work of the teacher. He must have a certificate granted by responsible authorities before he can enter the schoolroom. He must show professional growth while in service if he is to receive promotion or continue in the vocation.

Greater personal responsibility on church school teacher.--Naturally, all this is impossible with volunteer teachers who receive no pay for their services and are not employed under legal authority. No compulsion can be brought to bear; all must rest on the sense of duty and of opportunity of the individual teacher. Yet the Sunday school teacher needs even a more thorough background of preparation than the day-school teacher, for the work of instruction in the Sunday school is almost infinitely harder than in the day school. Religion and morals are more difficult to teach than arithmetic and geography. The church building usually lacks adequate classroom facilities. The lesson material is not as well graded and adapted to the children as the day-school texts. The lessons come but once a week, and the time for instruction is insufficient. The children do not prepare their lessons, and so come to the Sunday school lacking the mental readiness essential to receiving instruction.

This all means that the Sunday school teacher must rise to a sense of his responsibilities. He must realize that he holds a position of influence second to none in the spiritual development of his pupils. He must remember that he is dealing with a seed-time whose harvest involves the fruits of character and destiny. With these facts in mind he must ask himself whether he is justified in standing before his class as teacher without having given the time and effort necessary for complete preparation.

The teacher and his Bible.--The teacher should know his Bible. This means far more than to know its text and characters. The Bible is history, it is literature, it is a treatise on morals, it is philosophy, it is a repository of spiritual wisdom, it is a handbook of inspiration and guidance to the highest life man has in any age conceived.

To master the Bible one must have a background of knowledge of the life and history of its times. He must enter into the spirit and genius of the Hebrew nation, know their aspirations, their political and economic problems, and understand their tragedies and sufferings. He must know the historical and social setting of the Jewish people, the nations and civilizations that surrounded them, and the customs, mode of life, and trend of thought of contemporaneous peoples.

Not all of these things can be learned from the Bible itself. One must make use of the various helps and commentaries now available to Bible students. The religions of ancient Egypt, Assyria, Babylonia, Greece, and Rome should be studied. Ancient literatures should be placed under tribute, and every means employed to gain a working knowledge of the social medium out of which the Christian religion developed.

The teacher's knowledge of children.--Time was when we thought of the child as a miniature man, differing from adults on the physical side only in size and strength, and on the mental side only in power and grasp of thought. Now we know better. We know that the child differs from the adult not only in the *quantity* but also in the *quality* of his being.

It is the business of the teacher to understand how the child *thinks*. What is the child's concept of God? What is the character of the child's prayer? How does the child *feel* when he takes part in the acts of worship? We talk to the child about serving God; what is the child's understanding of service to God? We seek to train the child to loyalty to the church; what does the church stand for to the child? We teach the child about sin and forgiveness; just what is the child's comprehension of sin, and what does he understand by forgiveness? We tell the child that he must love God and the Christ; can a child control his affections as he will, or do they follow the trend of his thoughts and experiences? These are not idle questions. They are questions that must be answered by every teacher who would be more than the blind leader of the blind.

Coming to know the child.--How shall the teacher come to know the child? Professor George Herbert Palmer sets forth a great truth when he says that the first quality of a great teacher is the quality of *vicariousness*. By this he means the ability on the part of the teacher to step over in his imagination and take the place of the child. To look at the task with the child's mind and understanding, to feel the appeal of a lesson or story through the child's emotions, to confront a temptation with the child's power of will and self-control--this ability is the beginning of wisdom for those who would understand childhood. The teacher must first of all, therefore, be a sympathetic investigator in the laboratory of child life. Not only in the Sunday school, but daily, he must *observe, study, seek to interpret children*.

Nor should the teacher of religion neglect the books on the child and his religion. Many investigators are giving their time and abilities to studying child nature and child religion. A mastery of their findings will save us many mistakes in the leadership and training of children. A knowledge of their methods of study will show us how ourselves more intelligently to study childhood. Comprehension of the principles they represent, coupled with the results of our own direct interpretation of children, will convince us that, while each child differs from every other, *certain fundamental laws apply to all childhood*. It is the teacher's task and privilege to master these laws.

Knowledge of technique.--Teaching is an *art*, which must be learned the same as any other art. True, there are those who claim that anyone who knows a thing can teach it; but often the teacher who makes such a claim is himself the best refutation of its validity when he comes before his class. Probably most of us have known eminent specialists in their field of learning who were but indifferent teachers. It is not that they knew too much about their subjects, but that they had not mastered the art of its presentation to others.

The class hour is the teacher's great opportunity. His final measure as a teacher is taken as he stands before his class in the recitation. Here he succeeds or fails. In fact, here the whole system of religious education succeeds or fails. For it is in this hour, where the teacher meets his pupils face to face and mind to mind, that all else culminates. It is for this hour that the Sunday school is organized, the classrooms provided, and the lesson material prepared. It is in this hour that the teacher succeeds in kindling the interest, stirring the thought and feeling, and grounding the loyalty of his class. Or, failing in this, it is in the recitation hour that the teacher leaves the spiritual life of the child untouched by his contact with the Sunday school and so defeats its whole intent and purpose.

The teacher of religion should therefore ask himself: "What is my craftsmanship in instruction? Do I know how to *present* this material so that it will take hold upon my class? Do I know the technique of the recitation hour, and the principles of good teaching? Have I read what the scholars have written and what the experience of others has to teach me. Have I definitely planned and sought for skill? Is my work in the classroom the best that I can make it?"

The teacher must continuously be a student.--The successful teacher of religion must, therefore, be a student. He must continually grow in knowledge and in teaching power. There is no possibility of becoming "prepared" through the reading of certain books and the pursuit of certain courses of study and then having this preparation serve without further growth. The famous Dr. Arnold, an insatiable student until the day of his death, when asked why he found it necessary to prepare for each day's lessons, said he preferred that his pupils "should drink from a running stream rather than from a stagnant pool." This, then, should be the teacher's standard: *A broad background of general preparation, constant reading and study in the field of religion and religious teaching, special preparation for each lesson taught*.

The churches of each community should unite in providing a school for teacher training. Where the community training school cannot be organized, individual churches should organize training classes for their teachers. Such schools and classes have been provided in hundreds of places, and the movement is rapidly spreading. Wherever such opportunities are available the best church school teachers are flocking to the classes and giving the time and effort necessary to prepare for better service.

Even where no organized training classes are at present available, the earnest teacher can gain much help from following an organized course of reading in such lines as those just given. Excellent texts are available in most of these fields.

The reward.--One deep and abiding satisfaction may come to the teacher who feels the burden of reaching the standards set forth in this lesson. *It is all worth while*. Some make the mistake of charging against their task all the time, effort and devotion that go into preparing themselves as teachers of religion. But this is a false philosophy. For *a great work greatly performed leaves the stamp of its greatness on the worker*. All that we do toward making out of ourselves better teachers of childhood adds to our own spiritual equipment. All the study, prayer, and consecration we give to our work for the children returns a hundredfold to us in a richer experience and a larger capacity for service.

1. Recall several teachers whom you remember best from your own pupil days, and see whether you can estimate the qualities in their character or teaching which are responsible for the lasting impression.

2. Are you able to determine from the character chart which are your strongest qualities? Which are your weakest qualities? Just what methods are you planning to use to improve your personality?

3. In thinking of your class, are you able to judge in connection with different ones on what qualities of character they most need help? Are you definitely seeking to help on these points in your teaching?

4. Do you think that church-school teachers could pass as good an examination on what they undertake to teach as day-school teachers? Are the standards too high for day-school teachers? Are they high enough for church-school teachers?

5. Have you seen Sunday-school teachers at work who evidently did not know their Bibles? Have you seen others who seemed to know their Bibles but who were ignorant of childhood? Have you seen others whose technique of teaching might have been improved by a little careful study and preparation? Are you willing to apply these three tests to yourself?

FOR FURTHER READING
Palmer, The Ideal Teacher.
Hyde, The Teacher's Philosophy.
Slattery, Living Teachers.
Horne, The Teacher as Artist.

CHAPTER II
THE GREAT OBJECTIVE

All teaching has two objectives--the *subject* taught and the *person* taught. When we teach John grammar (or the Bible) we teach grammar (or the Bible), of course; but we also teach *John*. And the greater of these two objectives is John. It is easy enough to attain the lesser of the objectives. Anyone of fair intelligence can master a given amount of subject matter and present it to a class; but it is a far more difficult thing to understand the child--to master the inner secrets of the mind, the heart, and the springs of action of the learner.

Who can measure the potentialities that lie hidden in the soul of a child! Just as the acorn contains the whole of the great oak tree enfolded in its heart, so the child-life has hidden in it all the powers of heart and mind which later reach full fruition. Nothing is *created* through the process of growth and development. Education is but a process of unfolding and bringing into action the powers and capacities with which the life at the beginning was endowed by its Creator.

THE CHILD AS THE GREAT OBJECTIVE

The child comes into the world--indeed, comes into the school--with much potential and very little actual capital. Nature has through heredity endowed him with infinite possibilities. But these are but promises; they are still in embryonic form. The powers of mind and soul at first lie dormant, waiting for the awakening that comes through the touch of the world about and for the enlightenment that comes through instruction.

Given just the right touch at the opportune moment, and these potential powers spring into dynamic abilities, a blessing to their possessor and to the world they serve. Left without the right training, or allowed to turn in wrong directions, and these infinite capacities for good may become instruments for evil, a curse to the one who owns them and a blight to those against whom they are directed.

Children the bearers of spiritual culture.--The greatest business of any generation or people is, therefore, the education of its children. Before this all other enterprises and obligations must give way, no matter what their importance. It is at this point that civilization succeeds or fails. Suppose that for a single generation our children should, through some inconceivable stroke of fate, refuse to open their minds to instruction--suppose they should refuse to learn our science, our religion, our literature, and all the rest of the culture which the human race has bought at so high a price of sacrifice and suffering. Suppose they should turn deaf ears to the appeal of art, and reject the claims of morality, and refuse the lessons of Christianity and the Bible. Where then would all our boasted progress be? Where would our religion be? Where would modern civilization be? All would revert to primitive barbarism, through the failure of this one generation, and the race would be obliged to start anew the long climb toward the mountain top of spiritual freedom.

Each generation must therefore create anew in its own life and experience the spiritual culture of the race. Each child that comes to us for instruction, weak, ignorant, and helpless though he be, is charged with his part in the great program God has marked out for man to achieve. Each of these little ones is the bearer of an immortal soul, whose destiny it is to take its quality and form from the life it lives among its fellows. And ours is the dread and fascinating responsibility for a time to be the mentor and guide of this celestial being. Ours it is to deal with the infinite possibilities of child-life, and to have a hand in forming the character that this immortal soul will take. Ours it is to have the thrilling experience of experimenting in the making of a destiny!

Childhood's capacity for growth.--Nor must we ever think that because the child is young, his brain unripe, and his experience and wisdom lacking, our responsibility is the less. For the child's earliest impressions are the most lasting, and the earliest influences that act upon his life are the most powerful in determining its outcome. Remember that the babe, starting at birth with nothing, has in a few years learned speech, become acquainted with much of his immediate world, formed many habits which will follow him through life, and established the beginnings of permanent character and disposition. Remember the indelible impression of the bedside prayers of your mother, of the earliest words of counsel of your father, of the influence of a loved teacher, and then know that other children are to-day receiving their impressions from us, their parents and teachers.

Consider for a moment the child as he comes to us for instruction. We no longer insist with the older theologies that he is completely under the curse of "original sin," nor do we believe with certain sentimentalists that he comes "trailing clouds of glory." We believe that he has infinite capacities for good, and equally infinite capacities for evil, either of which may be developed. We know that at the beginning the child is sinless, pure of heart, his life undefiled. To know this is enough to show us our part. This is to lead the child aright until he is old enough to follow the right path of his own accord, to ground him in the motives and habits that tend to right living, and so to turn his mind, heart, and will to God that his whole being seeks accord with the Infinite.

Religious conservation.--If our leading of the child is wise, and his response is ready, there will be no falling away from a normal Christian life and a growing consciousness of God. This does not mean that the child will never do wrong, nor commit sin. It does not mean that the youth will not, when the age of choice has come, make a personal decision for Christ and consecrate his life anew to Christ's service. It means, rather, that the whole attitude of mind, and the complete trend of life of the child will be religious. It means that the original purity of innocence will grow into a conscious and joyful acceptance of the Christ-standard. It means that the child need never know a time when he is not within the Kingdom, and growing to fuller stature therein. It means that we should set our aim at *conservation* instead of reclamation as the end of our religious training.

Yet what a proportion of the energy of the church is to-day required for the reclaiming of those who should never have been allowed to go astray! Evangelistic campaigns, much of the preaching, "personal work," Salvation Army programs, and many other agencies are of necessity organized for the reclaiming of men and women who but yesterday were children in our homes and church schools, and plastic to our training. What a tragic waste of energy!--and then those who never return! Should we not be able more successfully to carry out the Master's injunction, "Feed my lambs"?

The child-Christian.--All of these considerations point to the inevitable conclusion that the child is the great objective of our teaching. Indeed, the child ought to be the objective of the work of the whole church. The saving of its children from wandering outside the fold is the supreme duty and the strategic opportunity of the church, standing out above all other claims whatever. We are in some danger of forgetting that when Jesus wanted to show his disciples the standard of an ideal Christian he "took a child and set him in the midst of them." We do not always realize that to *keep* a child a Christian is much more important than to reclaim him after he has been allowed to get outside the fold.

The recent report of a series of special religious meetings states that there were a certain number of conversions "exclusive of children," the implication being that the really important results were in the decisions of the adults. The same point of view was revealed when a church official remarked after the reception of a large group of new members, "It was an inspiring sight, *except that there were so few adults!"* When shall we learn that if we do our duty by the children there will be fewer adults left outside for the church to receive?

NO SUBJECT MATTER AN END IN ITSELF

The teacher must first of all take his stand with the child. He must not allow his attention and enthusiasms to become centered on the matter he teaches. He must not be satisfied when he has succeeded in getting a certain fact lodged in the minds of his pupils. He must first, last, and all the time look upon subject matter, no matter how beautiful and true it may be, as a *means* to an end. The end sought is certain desired changes in the life, thought, and experience of the child. There are hosts of teachers who can teach grammar (or the Bible), but comparatively *few who can teach John*.

This does not mean that the material we teach is unimportant, nor that we can fulfill our duty as teachers without the use of interesting, fruitful, and inspiring subject matter. It does not mean that we are not to love the subject we teach, and feel our heart thrill in response to its beauty and truth.

Making subject matter a means instead of an end.--One who is not filled with enthusiasm for a subject has no moral right to attempt to teach it, for the process will be dead and lifeless, failing to kindle the fires of response in his pupils and lacking in vital results. But the true teacher never loves a body of subject matter for its own sake; he loves it for what *through it* he can accomplish in the lives of those he teaches.

As a *student*, searching for the hidden meanings and thrilling at the unfolding beauties of some field of truth which we are investigating, we may love the thing we study for its own sake; and who of us does not feel in that way toward sections of our Bible, a poem, the record of noble lives, or the perfection of some bit of scientific truth? But when we face about and become the *teacher*, when our purpose is not our own learning but the teaching of another, then our attitude must change. We will then love our cherished body of material not less, but differently. We will now care for the thing we teach as an artisan cares for his familiar instruments or the artist cares for his brush--we will prize it as the *means through which* we shall attain a desired end.

Subject matter always subordinate to life.--It will help us to understand the significance of this fundamental principle if we pause to realize that all the matter we teach our children had its origin in human experience; it was first a part of human life. Our scientific discoveries have come out of the pressure of necessities that nature has put upon us, and what we now put into our textbooks first was *lived* by men and women in the midst of the day's activities. The deep thoughts, the beautiful sentiments, and the high aspirations expressed in our literature first existed and found expression in the lives of people. The cherished truths of our Bible and its laws for our spiritual development appeal to our hearts just because they have arisen from the lives of countless thousands, and so have the reality of living experience.

There is, therefore, no abstract truth for truth's sake. Just as all our culture material--our science, our literature, our body of religious truth--had its rise out of the experience of men engaged in the great business of living, so all this material must go back to life for its meaning and significance. The science we teach in our schools attains its end, not when it is learned as a group of facts, but when it has been *set at work* by those who learn it to the end that they live better, happier, and more fruitful lives. The literature we offer our children has fulfilled its purpose, not when they have studied the mechanism of its structure, read its pages, or committed to memory its lines, but when its glowing ideals and high aspirations have been *realized in the lives* of those who learn it.

And so this also holds for the Bible and its religious truth. Its rich lessons full of beautiful meaning may be recited and its choicest verses stored in the memory and still be barren of results, except as they are put to the test and find expression in living experience. The only true test of learning a thing is *whether the learner lives it*. The only true test of the value of what one learns is the extent to which it affects his daily life. The value of our teaching is therefore always to be measured by the degree to which it finds expression in the lives of our pupils. *John*, not grammar (nor even the Bible), is the true objective of our teaching.

EFFECT OF THE OBJECTIVE ON OUR TEACHING

Not only will this point of view vitalize our teaching for the pupils, but it will also save it from becoming commonplace and routine for ourselves. This truth is brought out in a conversation that occurred between an old schoolmaster and his friend, a business man.

The true objective saves from the rut of routine.--Said the business man, "Do you teach the same subjects year after year?"

The schoolmaster replied that he did.

"Do you not finally come to know this material all by heart, so that it is old to you?" asked the friend.

The schoolmaster answered that such was the case.

"And yet you must keep going over the same ground, class after class and year after year!" exclaimed the business man.

The schoolmaster admitted that it was so.

"Then," said his friend, "I should think that you would tire beyond endurance of the old facts, and grow weary beyond expression of repeating them after the charm of novelty and newness has gone. How do you live through the sameness and grind?"

"You forget one thing!" exclaimed the old schoolmaster, who had learned the secret of the *great objective*. "You forget that I am not really teaching that old subject matter at all; I am teaching *living boys and girls!* The matter I teach may become familiar. It may have lost the first thrill of novelty. But the *boys and girls are always new*; their hearts and minds are always fresh and inviting; their lives are always open to new impressions, and their feet ready to be turned in new directions. The old subject matter is but the means by which I work upon this living material that comes to my classroom from day to day. I should no more think of growing tired of it than the musician would think of growing tired of his violin."

And so the schoolmaster's friend was well answered.

Unsafe measures of success.--It is possible to lodge much subject matter in the mind which, once there, does not function. It is possible to teach many facts which play no part in shaping the ideals, quickening the enthusiasms, or directing the conduct. And all mental material which lies dead and unused is but so much rubbish and lumber of the mind. It plays no part in the child's true education, and it dulls the edge of the learner's interest and his enjoyment of the school and its instruction.

It is possible to have the younger children in our Sunday schools from week to week and still fail to secure sufficient hold on them so that they continue to come after they have reached the age of deciding for themselves. The proof of this is all too evident in the relatively small proportion of youth in our church school classes between the ages of fifteen and twenty-five.

It is possible to offer the child lessons from the Bible throughout all the years of childhood, and yet fail to ground sufficient interest in the Bible or religion so that in later years the man or woman naturally turns to the Bible for guidance or comfort, and fails to make religion the determining principle of the life.

The child the only true measure of success.--Let us therefore be sure of our objective. Let us never be proud nor satisfied that we have taught our class so much *subject matter*--so many facts, maxims, or lessons of whatever kind. We shall need to teach them all these things, and teach them well. But we must inquire further. We must ask, What have these things *done* for the boys and girls of my class? What has been the outcome of my teaching? How much effect has it had in life, character, conduct? In how far are my pupils different for having been in my class, and for the lessons I have taught them? In how far have I accomplished the ***true objective*** of my teaching?

Let us never feel secure merely because the children are found in the Sunday school, and because the statistical reports show increase in numbers and in average attendance. These things are all well; without them we cannot do the work which the church should do for its children. But these are but the externals, the outward signs. We must still inquire what real influence the school is having on the growing spiritual life of its children. We must ask what part our instruction is having in the making of Christians. We must measure all our success in terms of the child's response to our efforts. We must realize that we have failed except as we have caused the child's spiritual nature to unfold and his character to grow toward the Christ ideal.

1. As you think of your own teaching, are you able to decide whether you have been sufficiently clear in your objective? Have you rather ***assumed*** that if you presented the lessons as they came the results must of necessity follow, or have you been alive to the real effects on your pupils?

2. Are you able to discover definite changes that are working out in the lives of your pupils from month to month as you have them under your instruction? Are they more reverent, more truthful, more sure against temptation, increasingly conscious of God in their lives? What other effects might you look for?

3. Do you think that the church is in some degree overlooking its most strategic opportunity in not providing more efficiently for the religious education of its children? If more attention were given to religious nurture of children, would the problems of evangelism be less pressing, and a larger proportion of adults found in the church? What can the church school do to help? What can your class do?

4. Do you love the matter that you seek to teach the children? Do you love it for what it means to you, or for what through it you can do for them? Do you look upon the material you teach truly as a means and not as an end? Are you teaching subject matter or children?

5. Do you feel the real worth and dignity of childhood? Do you sometimes stop to remember that the ignorant child before you to-day may become the Phillips Brooks, the Henry Ward Beecher, the Livingstone, the Frances Willard, the Luther of to-morrow? Do you realize the responsibility that one takes upon himself when he undertakes to guide the development of a life?

6. Can you now make a statement of the measures that you will wish to apply to determine your degree of success as a teacher? It will be worth your while to try to make a list of the immediate objectives you will seek for your class to attain in their personal lives. Keep this list and see whether it is modified by the chapters that lie ahead.

FOR FURTHER READING
Harrison, A Study of Child Nature.
Moxcey, Girlhood and Character.
Dawson, The Child and His Religion.
Forbush, The Boy Problem.
Richardson (Editor), The American Home Series.
Richardson, Religious Education of Adolescents.

CHAPTER III
THE FOURFOLD FOUNDATION[1]

All good teaching rests on a fourfold foundation of principles. These principles are the same from the kindergarten to the university, and they apply equally to the teaching of religion in the church school or subjects in the day school. Every teacher must answer four questions growing out of these principles, or, failing to answer them, classify himself with the unworthy and incompetent. These are the four supreme questions:

1. What definite *aims* have I set as the goal of my teaching? What outcomes do I seek?

2. What *material*, or *subject matter*, will best accomplish these aims? What shall I stress and what shall I omit?

3. How can this material best be *organized*, or arranged, to adapt it to the child in his learning? How shall I plan my material?

4. What shall be my plan or *method of presentation* of this material to make it achieve its purpose? What of my technique of instruction?

---

1   The point of view and in some degree the outlines of this and several following chapters have been adapted from the author's text "Class-Room Method and Management," by permission of the publishers, *The Bobbs-Merrill Co.*, Indianapolis.

THE AIM IN TEACHING RELIGION

First of all, the teacher of religion must *have* an aim; he must know what ends he seeks to accomplish. Some statistically minded person has computed that, with all the marvelous accuracy of aiming modern guns, more than one thousand shots are fired for every man hit in battle. One cannot but wonder how many shots would be required to hit a man if the guns were not aimed at anything!

Is the analogy too strong? Is the teacher more likely than the gunner to reach his objective without consciously aiming at it? And can the teacher set up for attainment as definite aims as are offered the gunner? Do we *know* just what ends we seek in the religious training of our children?

Life itself sets the aim.--This much at least is certain. We know *where to look for* the aims that must guide us. We shall not try to formulate an aim for our teaching out of our own thought or reasoning upon the subject. We shall rather look out upon life, the life the child is now living and the later life he is to live, and ask: "What are the demands that life makes on the individual? What is the equipment this child will need as he meets the problems and tests of experience in the daily round of living? What qualities and powers will he require that he may the most fully realize his own potentialities and at the same time most fruitfully serve his generation? What abilities must he have trained in order that he may the most completely express God's plan for his life?" When we can answer such questions as these we shall have defined the aim of religious education and of our teaching.

The knowledge aim.--First of all, life demands *knowledge*. There are things that we must know if we are to avoid dangers and pitfalls. Knowledge shows the way, while ignorance shrouds the path in darkness. To be without knowledge is to be as a ship without a rudder, left to drift on the rocks and shoals. The religious life is intelligent; it must grasp, understand, and know how to use many great truths. To supply our children with *religious knowledge* is, therefore, one of the chief aims of our teaching.

Yet not all knowledge is of equal worth. Even religious knowledge is of all degrees of fruitfulness. Some knowledge, once acquired, fails to function. It has no point of contact with our lives. It does not deal with matters we are meeting in the day's round of experience. It therefore lies in the mind unused, or, because it is not used, it quickly passes from the memory and is gone. Such knowledge as this is of no real value. It is not worth the time and effort put upon its mastery; and it crowds out other and more fruitful knowledge that might take its place.

To be a true end of education, knowledge must be of such nature that it **can be put at work**. It must relate to actual needs and problems. It must have immediate and vital points of contact with the child's common experiences. The child must be able to see the relation of the truths he learns to his own interests and activities. He must feel their value and see their use in his work and in his play. This is as true of religious knowledge as of knowledge of other kinds. The religious knowledge the child needs, therefore, is a knowledge that **can at once be incorporated in his life**. To supply the child with knowledge of this vital, fruitful sort becomes, then, one great aim in the teaching of religion.

But knowledge alone is not enough. Indeed, knowledge is but the beginning of religious education, whereas we have been in danger of considering it the end. Many there are who **know** the ways of life but do not follow them. Many **know** the paths of duty, but choose an easier way. Many **know** the road to service and achievement, but do not enter thereon. If **to do** were as easy as to know what to do, then all of us would mount to greater heights.

The attitudes aim.--Life demands **goals** set ahead for achievement. It must have clearly defined the "worth whiles" which lead to endeavor. Along with the knowledge that guides our steps must be the impulses that drive to right action. Besides knowing what to do there must be inner compelling forces that **get things done**. The chief source of our goals and of the driving power within us is what, for want of a better term, we may call our **attitudes**.

Prominent among our attitudes are the **interests, enthusiasms, affections, ambitions, ideals, appreciations, loyalties, standards, and attachments** which predominate. These all have their roots set deep in our emotions; they are the measure of life's values. They are the "worth whiles" which give life its quality, and which define the goal for effort.

Chesterton tells us that the most important thing about any man is the **kind** *of philosophy he keeps*--that is to say, his **attitudes**. For it is out of one's attitudes that his philosophy of life develops, and that he settles upon the great aims to which he devotes himself. It is in one's attitudes that we find the springs of action and the incentives to endeavor. It is in attitudes that we find the forces that direct conduct and lead to character.

To train the intellect and store the mind with knowledge without developing a fund of right attitudes to shape the course of action is therefore even fraught with danger. The men in positions of political power who often misgovern cities or use public office as a means to private gain do not act from lack of knowledge or in ignorance of civic duty; their failure is one of ideals and loyalties; their attitude toward social trust and service to their fellow men is wrong. The men who use their power of wealth to oppress the poor and helpless, or unfairly exploit the labor of others to their own selfish advantage do not sin from lack of knowledge; their weakness lies in false standards and unsocial attitudes. Men and women everywhere who depart from paths of honor and rectitude fall more often from the lack of high ideals than because they do not know the better way.

The goal and the motive power in all such cases comes from a false philosophy of life; it is grounded in wrong attitudes. The education of those who thus misconceive life has failed of one of its chief aims--to develop right attitudes. Hence character is wanting.

The conduct, or application, aim.--The third and ultimate aim of education has been implied in the first two; it is **conduct, right living**. This is the final and sure test of the value of what we teach--how does it find **expression in action**? Do our pupils think differently, speak differently, act differently here and now because of what we teach them? Are they stronger when they meet temptation from day to day? Are they more sure to rise to the occasion when they confront duty or opportunity? Are their lives more pure and free from sin? Do the lessons we teach find expression in the home, in the school, and on the playground? Is there a real outcome *in terms of daily living*?

These are all fair questions, for knowledge is without meaning except as it becomes a guide to action. High ideals and beautiful enthusiasms attain their end only when they have eventuated in worthy deeds. What we *do* because of our training is the final test of its value. Conduct, performance, achievement are the ultimate measures of what our education has been worth to us. By this test we must measure the effects of our teaching.

Summary of the threefold aim.--The *aim* in teaching the child religion is therefore definite, even if it is difficult to attain. This aim may be stated in three great requirements which life itself puts upon the child and every individual:

1. *Fruitful knowledge*; knowledge of religious truths that can be set at work in the daily life of the child now and in the years that lie ahead.

2. *Right attitudes*; the religious warmth, responsiveness, interests, ideals, loyalties, and enthusiasms which lead to action and to a true sense of what is most worth while.

3. *Skill in living*; the power and will to use the religious knowledge and enthusiasms supplied by education in shaping the acts and conduct of the daily life.

True, we may state our aim in religious teaching in more general terms than these, but the meaning will be the same. We may say that we would lead the child to a knowledge of God as Friend and Father; that we seek to bring him into a full, rich experience of spiritual union with the divine; that we desire to ground his life in personal purity and free it from sin; that we would spur him to a life crowned with deeds of self-sacrifice and Christlike service; that we would make out of him a true Christian. This is well and is a high ideal, but in the end it sums up the results of the religious *knowledge, attitudes*, and *acts* we have already set forth as our aim. These are the parts of which the other is the whole; they are the immediate and specific ends which lead to the more distant and general. Let us, therefore, conceive our aim in *both* ways--the ideal Christian life as the final goal toward which we are leading, and the knowledge, attitudes, and acts that make up to-day's life as so many steps taken toward the goal.

SELECTING THE SUBJECT MATTER

After the aim the subject matter. When we would build some structure we first get plan and purpose in mind; then we select the material that shall go into it. It is so with education. Once we have set before us the aim we would reach, our next question is, What shall be the means of its attainment? When we have fixed upon the fruitful knowledge, the right attitudes, and the lines of conduct and action which must result from our teaching, we must then ask, What *means* shall we select to achieve these ends? What *material or subject matter* shall we teach in the church school?

The subject matter he presents is the instrumentality by which the teacher must accomplish his aims for his class. Through this material he must awaken thought, store the mind with vital truths, arouse new interests, create ideals and lead the life to God. As the artist works with brush and paint, with tool and clay, so the teacher must work with truths and lesson materials.

Guiding principles.--Two great principles must guide in the selection of subject matter for religious instruction:

1. *The material must be suited to the aims we seek.*

2. *The material must be adapted to the child.*

The tools and instruments the workman uses must be adapted to the purpose sought. Ask the expert craftsman what kind of plane or chisel you should buy for a piece of work you have in mind, and he will ask you just what ends you seek, what uses you would put them to. Ask the architect what materials you should have for the structure you would build, and he will tell you that depends on the plan and purpose of your building.

The material must fit the aim.--What materials of religious truth should the teacher bring to his class? The answer is that truths and lessons must be suited to the aim we seek. Would we lead our children to understand the Fatherhood of God and to love him for his tender care? Then the lessons must contain this thought, and not be built on irrelevant material. Would we lead youth to catch the thrill and inspiration of noble lives, to pattern conduct after worthy deeds? Then our lesson material must deal with the high and fine in character and action, and not with trivial things of lesser value.

So also, if we would capture the interest of childhood for the church school and bind its loyalty to the church, the subject matter we offer and the lessons we teach in the house of God must contain the glow and throb of life, and not be dry and barren. If we would awaken religious feeling and link the emotions to God, we must not teach empty lessons, meaningless dates, and musty facts that fail to reach the heart because they have no inner meaning.

Small use to set high aims and then miss them for want of material suited for their attainment. Small use to catalogue the fine qualities of heart and mind we would train in our children and then fail of our aim because we choose wrong tools with which to work. Not all facts found in the Bible are of equal worth to children, nor are all religious truths of equal value. Nothing should be taught *just because it is true*, nor even because it is found in the Bible. The final question is whether this lesson material is the best we can choose for the child himself; whether it will give him the knowledge he can use, train the attitudes he requires, and lead to the acts and conduct that should rule his life.

The material must fit the child.--The subject matter we teach *must also be fitted to the child*. It must be within his grasp and understanding. We do not feed strong meat to babes. What may be the grown person's meat may be to the child poison. It does no good to load the mind with facts it cannot comprehend. There is no virtue in truths, however significant and profound, if they are beyond the reach of the child's experience. Matter which is not assimilated to the understanding is soon forgotten; or if retained, but weighs upon the intellect and dulls its edge for further learning.

There can be little doubt that we have quite constantly in most of our Sunday schools forced upon the child no small amount of matter that is beyond his mental grasp, and so far outside his daily experience that it conveys little or no meaning. We have over-intellectualized the child's religion. Jesus was "to the Greeks foolishness" because they had no basis of experience upon which to understand his pure and unselfish life. May not many of the facts, figures, dates, and events from an ancient religion which we give young children likewise be to them but foolishness! May not the lessons upon some of the deepest, finest and most precious concepts in our religion, such as faith, atonement, regeneration, repentance, the Trinity, be lost or worse than lost upon our children because we force them upon unripe minds and hearts at an age when they are not ready for them?

Let us then, ***not forget the child*** when we teach religion! Let us not assume that truths and lessons are an end in themselves. Let us constantly ask, as we prepare our lessons, Will this material work as a true leaven in the life? Will it take root and blossom into character, fine thought, and worthy conduct? While our children dumbly ask for living bread let us not give them dead stones and dry husks, which cannot feed their souls! Let us adapt our subject matter to the child.

The use of stress and neglect.--That the lesson material printed in the Sunday school booklets is not always well adapted to the children every teacher knows. But there it is, and what can we do but teach it, though it may sometimes miss the mark?

There is one remedy the wise and skillful teacher always has at his command. By the use of ***stress*** and ***neglect*** the matter of the lesson may be made to take quite different forms. The points that are too difficult may be omitted or but little emphasized. The matter that best fits the child may be stressed and its application made. Illustrations, stories, and lessons from outside sources may be introduced to suit the aim. Great truths may be restated in terms within childhood's comprehension. The true teacher, like the craftsman, will select now this tool, now that to meet his purpose. Regardless of what the printed lesson offers, he will reject or use, supplement or replace with new material as the needs of his class may demand. The true teacher will be the master, and not the servant, of the subject matter he uses.

HOW SHALL WE ORGANIZE AND PLAN THE LESSONS?

When the *content* of the subject matter has been decided upon then comes its *organization*. How shall we arrange and plan the material we teach so as to give the children the easiest and most natural mode of approach to its learning?

The great law here is that *the arrangement of subject matter must be psychological*. This only means that we must always ask ourselves how will the child most easily and naturally enter upon the learning of this material? How can I organize it for the recitation so that it will most strongly appeal to his interest? How can I arrange it so that it will be most easily grasped and understood? How can I plan the lesson so that its relation to immediate life and conduct will be most clear and its application most surely made?

The psychological mode of approach.--I recently happened into a junior Sunday school class where the lesson was on faith. The teacher evidently did not know how to plan for a psychological mode of approach to this difficult concept. He began by defining faith in Paul's phrase as "the substance of things hoped for; the evidence of things not seen." He then went to the dictionary definition, which shows the relation of faith to belief. He discussed the relation of faith to works, as presented in the writings of James. But all to no avail. The class was uninterested and inattentive. The lesson did not take hold. The time was wasted and the opportunity lost. I excused myself and went to another classroom.

Here they had the same topic. But the teacher had sought for and found a starting point from which to explain the meaning of faith in terms that the children could understand. The teacher's eye rested for a moment on John; then: "John, when does your next birthday come?"

"The sixteenth of next month," replied John promptly.

"Going to get any presents, do you think?" asked the teacher.

"Yes, sir," answered John with conviction.

"What makes you think so?" inquired the teacher. "Not everybody does receive birthday presents, you know."

"But I am sure I will," persisted John. "You see, I know my father and mother. They have never yet let one of my birthdays pass without remembering me, and I am sure they are not going to begin to forget me now. They think too much of me."

"You seem to have a good deal of *faith* in your father and mother," remarked the teacher.

"Well I guess I *have!*" was John's enthusiastic response.

And right at this point the way was wide open to show John and the class the meaning of faith in a heavenly Father. The wise teacher had found a *point of contact* in John's faith in the love and care of his parents, and it was but a step from this to the broader and deeper faith in God.

It is a law of human nature that we are all interested first of all in what affects our own lives. Our attention turns most easily to what relates to or grows out of our own experience. The *immediate and the concrete* are the natural and most effective starting points for our thought. The distant and remote exert little appeal to our interest; it is the near that counts. Especially do these rules hold for children.

Making sure of a point of contact.--All these facts point the way for the teacher in the planning and organization of material for his class. The point of departure must always be sought in some *immediate interest or activity in the life of the child*, and not in some abstract truth or far-away lesson, however precious these may be to the adult Christian. And no lesson is ready for presentation until the way into the child's interest and comprehension has been found. Many a lesson that might have been full of rich spiritual meaning for the child has been lost to our pupils because it was presented out of season, or because the vital connection between the truth and the child's experience was not discovered by the teacher.

This principle suggests that in the main children should not be taught religious truths in terms which they cannot grasp, nor in such a way that the application to their own lives is not clear. For example, the vital truths contained in the church catechisms are not for children; the statement of them is too abstract and difficult, and the meaning too remote from the child's experience. Many of the same truths can be presented to children in the form of stories or illustrations; other of the truths may rest until the child becomes older before claiming his attention. Bible verses and sentiments completely outside the child's comprehension are not good material for memorizing. Lessons upon the more difficult concepts and deeper problems of religion belong to the adult age, and should not be forced upon children.

Our guiding principle, therefore, is to *keep close to the mind, heart, and daily life of childhood.* Then *adapt the subject matter we teach to the mind, interests, and needs of those we teach.* Definitions, rules, abstract statements, general truths have little or no value with children. It is the story, the concrete incident, the direct application growing out of their own experiences that takes hold.

PRESENTING THE LESSON--INSTRUCTION

After the aim has been clearly conceived, and after the lesson material has been wisely chosen and properly organized, there still remains the most important part--that of "getting the lesson across" to the class. Many a valuable lesson, full of helpfulness, has been lost to the pupils because the teacher lacked the power to bring his class to the right pitch for receiving and retaining impressions. Many a class period has been wasted because the teacher failed to present the material of the lesson so that it gripped interest and compelled attention.

Response a test of instruction.--The *first* test of good instruction is the *response of the class*. Are the children alert? Are they keen for discussion, or for listening to stories told or applications made? Do they think? Do they enjoy the lesson hour, and give themselves happily and whole-heartedly to it? Is their conduct good, and their attitude serious, reverent, and attentive? Are they all "in the game," or are there laggards, inattentive ones, and mischief-makers?

These questions are all crucial. For the first law of all learning is *self-activity*. There is no possibility of teaching a child who is not mentally awake. Only the active mind grasps, assimilates, remembers, applies. The birth of new ideas, the reaching of convictions, the arriving at decisions all come in moments of mental stress and tension. Lethargy of thought and feeling is fatal to all classroom achievement. Therefore, no matter how keenly alert the teacher's mind may be, no matter how skillful his analysis of an important truth may be if his class sit with flagging interest and lax attention.

Results a test of instruction.--The *second* test of good instruction is our skill in handling the material of the lesson, and *shaping the trend of thought and discussion*. Are the children interested in the right things? Are the central truths of the lesson being brought out and applied? Is the discussion centered on topics set for our consideration, or does it degenerate into aimless talk on matters of personal or local interest which have no relation to the lesson? In short, does the recitation period yield the *fruitful knowledge* we had set as a goal for this lesson? Does it stimulate the *attitudes* and motives we had meant to reach? Does it lead to the *applications* in life and conduct which were intended? *Does it get results?*

The four points of this lesson are of supreme importance in teaching religion. The *aim* must be clear, definite, and possible of attainment. The *subject matter* of instruction must be wisely selected as an instrument for reaching the aim set forth. The *organization* of this material must adapt it to the mind and needs of the child. The *presentation* of the lesson material in the recitation must be such that its full effect is brought to bear upon the mind and heart of those we teach.

Each of these four points will be further elaborated in the chapters which follow. In fact, the remainder of the text is chiefly a working out and applying of these fundamental principles to the teaching of religion.

1. To what extent would you say you have been directing your teaching toward a definite aim? Just how does the problem of this chapter relate itself to the preceding chapter on the "Great Objective"?

2. Do you think the majority of those who have come up through the church school possess as full and definite a knowledge of the Bible and the fundamentals of religion as we have a right to expect? If not, where is the trouble and what the remedy?

3. Have you been consciously emphasizing the creation of right attitudes as one of the chief outcomes of your teaching? Do you judge that you are as successful in the developing of religious attitudes as in imparting information? If not, can you find a

remedy?

4. To what extent do you think your instruction is actually carrying over into the immediate life and conduct of your class in their home, school, etc.? If not to so great an extent as you could wish, are you willing to make this one of the great aims of your teaching from this time on, seeking earnestly throughout this text and in other ways to learn how this may be done?

5. Do you on the whole feel that the subject matter you are teaching your pupils is adapted to the aims you seek to reach in their lives? If not, how can you supplement and change to make it more effective? Have you a broad enough knowledge of such material yourself so that you can select material from other sources for them?

6. To what extent do you definitely plan each lesson for the particular children you teach so as to make it most accessible to their interest and grasp? Do you plan each lesson to secure a psychological mode of approach? How do you know when you have a psychological approach?

FOR FURTHER READING
Betts, Class-Room Method and Management, Part I.
Coe, A Social Theory of Religious Education, Part II.
DuBois, The Point of Contact in Teaching.

CHAPTER IV
RELIGIOUS KNOWLEDGE OF MOST WORTH

The child comes into the world devoid of all knowledge and understanding. His mind, though at the beginning a blank, is a potential seedbed in which we may plant what teachings we will. The babe born into our home to-day can with equal ease be made into a Christian, a Buddhist, or a Mohammedan. He brings with him the instinct to respond to the appeal religion makes to his life, but the kind and quality of his religion will depend largely on the religious atmosphere he breathes and the religious ideas and concepts placed in his mind through instruction and training.

What, then, shall we teach our children, in religion? If fruitful knowledge is to be one of the chief aims of our teaching, *what* knowledge shall we call fruitful? What are the great foundations on which a Christian life must rest? Years ago Spencer wrote a brilliant essay on ***knowledge of most worth*** in the field of general education. What knowledge is of most worth in the field of religious education? For not all knowledge, as we have seen, is of equal value. Some religious knowledge is fruitful because it ***can be set at work*** to shape our attitudes and guide our acts; other religious knowledge is relatively fruitless because it ***finds no point of contact*** with experience.

To answer our question we must therefore ask: "What knowledge will serve to guide the child's foot-steps aright from day to day as he passes through his childhood? What truths will even now, while he is still a child, awaken his spiritual appreciation and touch the springs of his emotional response to the heavenly Father? What religious concepts, once developed, will lead the youth into a rich fullness of personal experience and develop in him the will and capacity to serve others? What religious knowledge will finally make most certain a life of loyalty to the church and the great cause for which it stands?" When we can answer these questions we shall then be able to say what knowledge is of most worth in the religious training of our children.

THE CHILD'S CONCEPT OF GOD

The child must come to know about God, even as a little child. Long before he can understand about *religion*, he can learn about a heavenly Father. This does not imply that the child (or that we ourselves!) can know God in any full or complete way. Indeed, a God who could be known in his entirety by even the deepest and wisest finite mind would be no God at all. Yet everyone must give some meaning to God. Everyone does have some more or less definite idea, image, or mental picture of the God he thinks about, prays to, and worships.

The child's idea of God develops gradually.--We need not be concerned that God does not mean the same to the child with his mental limitations that he means to us. Meaning comes only out of experience, and this will grow. The great thing is that the child's fundamental concept of God shall start right, that in so far as it goes it shall be essentially true, and that it shall be clear and definite enough to guide his actions. More than this we cannot ask for; less than this does not give the child a God real enough to be a vital factor and an active force in his life.

It is to be expected, then, that the child's earliest concepts of God will be faulty and incomplete, and that in many points they will later need correction. Probably most children first think of God as having human form and attributes; the idea of spirit is beyond their grasp. God is to them a kind of magnified and glorified Father after the type of their earthly father. This need not concern us if we make sure that the crude beginnings of the God-idea have no disturbing elements in them, and that as the concept grows it moves in the right direction.

The harm from false concepts.--Mr. H.G. Wells[2] bitterly complains against the wrong concept of God that was allowed to grow in his mind as a child. These are his words: "He and his hell were the nightmare of my childhood.... I thought of him as

2   God the Invisible King, p. 44.

a fantastic monster perpetually waiting to condemn and to strike me dead!... He was over me and about my silliness and forgetfulness as the sky and sea would be about a child drowning in mid-Atlantic." It was only as the child grew into youth, and was able to discard this false idea of God that he came to feel right toward him.

The harm done a child by false and disturbing concepts of God is hard to estimate. A small boy recently came home from Sunday school and confided to his mother that he "didn't think it was fair for God to spy on a fellow!" A sympathetic inquiry by the mother revealed the fact that the impression brought from the lesson hour was of God keeping a lookout for our wrongdoings and sins, and constantly making a record of them against us, as an unsympathetic teacher might in school. The beneficent and watchful oversight and care of God had not entered into the concept.

It is clear that with this wrong understanding of God's relation to him the child's attitude and the response of his heart toward God could not be right. The lesson hour which left so false an impression of God in the child's mind did him lasting injury instead of good.

How wrong concepts may arise.--Pierre Loti tells in his reminiscences of his own child-life how he went out into the back yard and threw stones at God because it had rained and spoiled the picnic day. In his teaching, God had been made responsible for the weather, and the boy had come to look upon prayer as a means of getting what he wanted from God. It took many years of experience to rid the child's mind of the last vestiges of these false ideas. The writer recalls a troublesome idea of God that inadvertently secured lodgment in his own mind through the medium of a picture in his first geography. In the section on China was the representation of a horrid, malignant looking idol underneath which was printed the words, "A God." For many years the image of this picture was associated with the thought of God, and made it hard to respond to the concept of God's beauty, goodness, and kindness.

Wrong concepts of God may leave positive antagonisms which require years to overcome. A little girl of nearly four years had just lost her father. She did not understand the funeral and the flowers and the burial. She came to her mother in the evening and asked where her papa was. The stricken mother replied that "God had taken him."

"But when is he coming back?" asked the child.

The mother answered that he could not come back.

"Not ever?" persisted the child.

"Not ever," whispered the mother.

"Won't God let him?" asked the relentless questioner.

The heart-broken mother hesitated for a word of wisdom, but finally answered, "No, God will not let him come back to us."

Care and wisdom needed.--And in that moment the harm was done. The child had formed a wrong concept of God as one who would willfully take away her father and not let him return. She burst out in a fit of passion: "I don't like God! He takes my papa and keeps him away."

That night she refused to say her prayer, and for weeks remained rebellious and unforgiving toward the God whom she accused of having robbed her of her father. How should the mother have answered her child's question? I cannot tell in just what words, but the words in which we answer the child's questions must be chosen with such infinite care and wisdom that bitterness shall not take the place which love toward God should occupy in the heart.

Another typical difficulty is that children are often led to think of God as a distant God. A favorite Sunday school hymn sings of "God above the great blue sky." To many children God is "in heaven," and heaven is localized at an immeasurable distance. Hence the fact of God's nearness is wholly missed. Children come to think of God as seated on a great white throne, an aged, austere, and severe Person, more an object of fear than of love. And then we tell the children that they "must love God," forgetting that love never comes from a sense of duty or compulsion, but springs, when it appears, spontaneously from the heart because it is compelled by lovable traits and appealing qualities in the one to be loved!

The concept of God which the child needs.--The concept of God which the child first needs, therefore, is God as loving Father, expecting obedience and trust from his children; God as inviting Friend; God as friendly Protector; God ever near at hand; God who can understand and sympathize with children and enter into their joys and sorrows; God as Creator, in the sunshine and the flowers; but above all, God filling the heart with love and gladness. The concept which the child needs of Jesus is of his surpassing goodness, his unselfish courage, and his loving service.

All religious teaching which will lead to such concepts as these is grounding the child in knowledge that is rich and fruitful, for it is making God and Christ *real* to him. All teaching which leads to false concepts is an obstacle in the way of spiritual development.

THE CHILD'S CONCEPT OF RELIGION

Gradually throughout his training the child should be forming a clear concept of religion and the part it is to play in the life. This cannot come through any formal definition, nor through any set of precepts. It must be a growth, stimulated by instruction, guided by wise counsel, given depth of meaning through the lives of strong men and women who express the Christian ideal in their daily living.

Matthew Arnold tells us that religion is "morality lit up by emotion." We turn to God for our inspiration, for the quickening of our motives, for fellowship, communion and comfort; but it is when we face the duties and relationships of the day's work and its play that we prove how close we have been to God and what we have received from him. As there can be no religion without God, neither can there be religion without morality; that is, without righteous living.

Connecting religion with life.--One of the chief aims in teaching the child religion should therefore be to ground him in the understanding that *religion is life*. Probably no greater defect exists in our religion to-day than our constant tendency to divorce it from life. There are many persons who undertake to divide their lives up into compartments, one for business, one for the relations of the home, one for social matters, one for recreation and amusement, and *one for religion*. They make the mistake of assuming that they can keep these sections of the life separate and distinct from each other, forgetting that life is a unity and that the quality of each of its aspects inevitably colors and gives tone to all the rest.

The child should be saved the comfortable assumption so tragically prevalent that religion is chiefly a matter for Sundays; that it consists largely in belonging to the church and attending its services; that it finds its complete and most effective expression in the observance of certain rites and ceremonials; that we can serve God without serving our fellow men; that creeds are more important than deeds; that saying "Lord, Lord," can take the place of a ministry of service.

Religion defined in noble living.--There is only one way to save the child from such crippling concepts as these: that is to hold up to him the challenge of *life at its best and noblest*, to show him the effects of *religion at work*. What are the qualities we most admire in others? What are the secrets of the influence, power, and success of the great men and women whose names rule the pages of history? What are the attributes that will draw people to us as friends and followers and give us power to lead them to better ways? What are the things that will yield the most satisfaction, and that are most worth while to seek and achieve as the outcome of our own lives? What is true success, and how shall we know when we have achieved it? *Why does the Christ, living his brief, modest, and uneventful life and dying an obscure and tragic death, stand out as the supreme model and example for men to pattern their lives by?*

These are questions that the child needs to have answered, not in formal statements, of course, but in terms that will reach his understanding and appreciation. These are truths that he needs to have lodged in his mind, so that they may stir his imagination, fire his ambition, and harden his will for endeavor. These are the goals that the child needs to have set before him as the measure of success in life, the pathways into which his feet should be directed.

The qualities religion puts into the life.--What, then, are the things men live by? What are the great qualities which have ruled the finest lives the world has known? How does religion express itself in the run of the day's experience? What are some of the objective standards by which religion is to be measured in our own lives or in the lives of others, in the lives of children or in the lives of adults? What are the characterizing features in the life and personality of Jesus? What did he put first in practice as well as in precept?

Joyousness. No word was oftener on the lips of Jesus than the word "joy," and the world has never seen such another apostle of joyousness. The life that lacks joy is flat for him who lives it, and exerts little appeal to others.

Good will. The good will of Jesus embraces all manner and conditions of people. His magnanimity and generosity under all conditions were one of the charms of his personality and one of the chief sources of his strength.

Service. Jesus's life was, if possible, more wonderful than his death, and nothing in his life was more wonderful than his passion for serving others. The men and women whom the world has remembered and honored in all generations and among all peoples are the men and women who found their greatness in service.

Loyalty. Steadfastness to the cause he had espoused led Jesus to the cross. Great characters do not ask what road is easy, but what way is right. Where duty leads, the strong do not falter nor fail, cost what it may. They see their task through to the end, though it mean that they die.

Sympathy. Jesus always understood. His heart had eyes to see another's need. His love was as broad as the hunger of the human heart for comradeship. We are never so much our best selves as when self is forgotten, and we enter into the joys or the sorrows of one who needs us.

Purity. Sin has its price for all it gives us. We cannot stain our souls and find them white again. We later reap whatever now we sow. Jesus's life of righteousness, lived amid temptations such as we all meet, is a challenge to every man who would be the captain of his own soul.

Sincerity. No man ever doubted that Jesus meant what he said. No man ever accused him of acting a part. His enemies, even, never found him misrepresenting or speaking other than the truth. All truly fine characters can be trusted for utter sincerity of word, of purpose, and of deed.

Courage. Jesus was never more sublime than under conditions that test men's courage. Did he face hostile mob and servile judge? did he find himself misunderstood and deserted by those who had been his friends? must he bid his disciples a last farewell? did he see the shadow of the cross over his pathway?--yet he never faltered. His courage stood all tests.

Vision. A distinguishing quality of the great is their power to put first things first. Jesus possessed a fine sense of values. He willingly sold all he had that he might buy the pearl of great price. His temptations to follow after lesser values left him unscathed, and he refused to command the stones to be made bread, or to do aught else that would turn him from his mission.

God-Consciousness. Those who have most left their impress upon the world and the hearts of men have not worked through their own power alone. They have known how to link their lives to the infinite Source of power; the way has been open between their lives and God. Jesus never for a moment doubted that all the resources of God were at his command, hence he had but to reach out and they were his.

*   *   *   *   *

It is evident, as before stated, that this functional definition of religion, this great program of living, cannot be thrust on the child all at once--cannot be *thrust* on him at all. But day after day and year after year throughout the period of his training the conviction should be taking shape in the child's mind that these are the *real* things of life, the truest measure of successful living, the highest goals for which men can strive. The definition of religion which he forms from his instruction should be broad enough to include these values and such others of similar kind as Christianity at its best demands.

KNOWLEDGE OF THE BIBLE

A knowledge of the essential parts of the *Bible* is indispensable to Christian culture. The Bible is the storehouse of spiritual wisdom of the ages, the matchless textbook of religion. Great men and women of all generations testify to its power as a source of inspiration and guidance. To be ignorant of its fundamental spiritual truths is to lack one of the chiefest instruments of religious growth and development. Not to know its teachings is to miss the strongest and best foundation that has ever been laid for fruitful and happy living. To lose a knowledge of the Bible out of our lives is to deprive ourselves of the ethical and religious help needed to redeem society and bring the individual to his rightful destiny. Yet this generation is confronted by a widespread and universal ignorance of the Bible, even among the adherents of the churches.

Making the Bible useful to the child. The child cannot be taught all of the Bible as a child. Indeed, parts of if dealing with the ideals and practices of peoples and times whose primitive standards were far below those of our own times are wholly unsuited to the mind of childhood, and should be left until maturity has given the mental perspective by which to interpret them. Other parts of the Bible prove dry and uninteresting to children, and are of no immediate spiritual significance to them. Still other parts, which later will be full of precious meaning, are beyond the grasp or need of the child in his early years and should be left for a later period. But with all these subtractions there still remains a rich storehouse of biblical material suited for all ages from earliest childhood to maturity. This material should be assembled and arranged in a ***children's Bible***. This abridged Bible should then be made a part of the mental and spiritual possession of every child.

The knowledge of the Bible which will be of most worth to the child must be a ***functioning*** knowledge; a knowledge that can and will be put at work in the child's thought, helping him form his judgments of right and wrong and arrive at a true sense of moral values; a knowledge that stirs the soul's response to the appeal God makes to the life; a knowledge that daily serves as a guide to action amid the perplexities and temptations that are met; a knowledge that lives and grows as the years pass by, constantly revealing deeper meanings and more significant truths.

The test of useful knowledge.--This is all to say that the knowledge of the Bible given the child must in no sense be a merely formal knowledge, a knowledge of so many curious or even interesting facts separated from their vital meaning and application. It must not consist of truths which for the most part ***do not influence thought and action***. Not how many facts are lodged in the mind, nor how many have passed through the mind and been forgotten, but ***how many truths are daily being built into character***--this measures the value of the knowledge we teach the child from the Bible.

KNOWLEDGE ABOUT THE CHURCH

The church represents religion organized. Because of our social impulses we need to worship together in groups. Many religious activities, such as education, evangelism, missionary enterprises, and reforms, can be successfully carried out only by joint action; hence we have the church, a ***means of religious culture***, and the ***instrument of religious service***. Few there are who, outside the church, maintain their own religious experience or carry the ministry of religious service to others. A knowledge of the church is therefore an essential part of the child's religious education.

What the child needs to know about the church.--This does not mean that the child needs to know the technical and detailed history of the Christian Church; this may come later. Nor does it mean that the child needs to know the different theological controversies through which the church has passed and the creeds that have resulted; this also may come later. What the child needs first to know is that the church is the instrument of religion, the home of religious people; that the Christian Church began with the followers of Jesus, and that it has existed ever since; that it has done and is doing much good in the world; that the best and noblest men and women of each generation work with and through the church; that the church is worthy of our deepest love and appreciation, and that it should command our fullest loyalty and support.

Besides this rather general knowledge of the church, the child should know the organization and workings of the present-day church. He should come to know as much of its program, plans, and ideals as his age and understanding will permit.

Even the younger children are able to understand and sympathize with the missionary work of the church, both in home and in foreign lands. Missionary instruction offers a valuable opportunity to quicken the religious imagination and broaden the social interests. Lessons showing the church at work in missionary fields should therefore be freely brought to the child.

Knowledge of the church's achievements.--The part the church has taken and is to-day taking in advancing the cause of education will appeal to the child's admiration and respect. A knowledge of its philanthropies will make a good foundation for the later loyalties to be developed toward the church as an institution. The important influence of the church in furthering moral reforms and social progress is well within the appreciation of adolescents, and should be brought to their recognition.

Especially should children know the activities of their own local church; they should learn of its different organizations and of the work each is doing; they should know its financial program--where the money comes from and the uses to which it is put; they should know its plans ahead in so far as their participation can be used in carrying out its activities. All these lines of information are necessary to the child in order that his interest and loyalty may have an intelligent and enduring basis.

Knowledge of one's own church.--The first knowledge of the church as an institution given the child should be of the **church as a whole**, and should have no denominational bias. We should first aim to make out of our children **Christians**, and only later to make out of them Methodists, Presbyterians, Baptists, or Congregationalists.

There comes a time, however, when the child should become informed concerning his own particular church or denomination. He should learn of its history, its achievements, its creeds, its plan of organization and polity. This is not with the purpose of cultivating a narrow sectarianism, but in the interests of a self-respecting intelligence concerning the particular branch of the church which is one's spiritual home. That the great mass of our people to-day possess any reasonable fund of knowledge about the Christian Church or their own denomination may well be doubted. This is a serious fault in religious education.

KNOWLEDGE OF RELIGIOUS MUSIC AND ART

Not all of the child's religious impressions come through direct instruction in the facts and precepts of religion. Religious feeling and comprehension of the deeper meanings and values often best spring from their expression in music and art.

Music essential to religion.--No other form of expression can take the place of music in creating a spirit of reverence and devotion, or in inspiring religious feeling. So closely is music interwoven with religion that no small part of the world's greatest musical masterpieces have a religious motive as their theme. Even among primitive peoples music is an important feature of religious ceremonials. The Christian Church has a large and growing body of inspiring hymnology.

The child needs to be led into a knowledge of religious music. He needs this knowledge as a stimulus and a means of expression for his own spiritual life. But he also needs it in order to take part in the exercises of his church and its organizations. He needs it in order to enjoy music and do his part in producing it in the home and the school. This means that children should come to know the hymnology of the church; they should know the words and the music of such worthy and inspiring hymns as are adapted to their age and understanding. They should finally, during the course of their development to adulthood, learn to know and enjoy the great religious oratorios and other forms of musical expression.

The place of art in religion.--Art, like music, owes much of its finest form and development to religion. Religious hope, aspiration, and devotion have always sought expression in pictorial or plastic art and in noble architecture. We owe it to our children to put them in possession of this rich spiritual heritage. They should know and love the great masterpieces of painting dealing with religious themes. They should not only have these as a part of their instruction in the church school classes, but they should also have them in their homes and in their schools, and see them in public art galleries and in other public buildings suitable for their display.

Wherever possible the church building should in its architecture express in a worthy way the religious ideals of its members. It should first of all be adapted to the uses expected of it. It should be beautiful in conception and execution, and should allow no unlovely or unworthy elements to enter into its structure.

We should teach our children something of the wonder and beauty of religious architecture as represented in the great cathedrals and churches of all lands, and lead them to see in these creations the desire and attempt of great souls to express their appreciation for God's goodness to men.

1. It will help you to understand the child's idea of God if you will think back to your own childhood and answer the following questions: Just who and what was God to you? Was he near by or far off? When you prayed, to what kind of a Being was the prayer addressed? Did Jesus seem more near and friendly to you than God? What were (or are) the most outstanding attributes of God's nature to you? Did you ever have any disturbing ideas about God?

2. Now, suppose you attempt to answer these same questions about the children in your class. You will have to remember that the child may not be able to explain just what God seems to him--perhaps you can hardly do this yourself. Further, a child may often have some notion that what he feels is queer or would not be well received, and hence he will not fully express it to others.

3. Just what does religion seem to you to be? Is it largely a way of living or a set of conventions and restraints? How did religion appeal to you in your childhood? Are you able to tell how the children of your class understand religion? What definite help are you giving them toward broadening and enriching their concept of religion? Are you leading them to see that religion is a way of living the day's life?

4. To what extent do you feel that you really know the Bible? Could you give a sketch of twenty of its leading characters, describing the strengths and weaknesses of character of each? Could you describe the great biblical events, and draw the lessons they teach? Could you compare and characterize the Hebrew religion and the religion of Jesus? Are the pupils in your class going to be able from the work of the church school to answer favorably these and similar questions?

5. We expect good citizens to know something of the history of their country and their commonwealth. Is it too much to ask members of the Christian Church to have the same information about the church? Could you pass a fair examination on the history and achievements of the church? Of your own particular church? Are the children of your church school growing in this knowledge? The children of your class?

6. To what extent do the children of your class know the hymns of the church? Is care taken to give them such hymns as are suited to their age? Are worthy hymns taught them, or the silly rimes found in many church song books? (This does not mean that children should be taught music beyond their comprehension; there is much good music suited to different ages.) Are your children having an opportunity to know the great religious pictures? Religious architecture? (Here also the work must be adapted to the age.)

FOR FURTHER READING

Coe, Education in Religion and Morals.

Brown, The Modern Man's Religion, chapter on "The Use of the Bible."

Fosdick, The Manhood of the Master.

Weld and Conant, Songs for Little People.

Bailey, The Gospel in Art.

CHAPTER V
RELIGIOUS ATTITUDES TO BE CULTIVATED

Life never stands still; especially does the life of the child never stand still. It is always advancing, changing, reconstructing. Starting with an unripe brain, and with no fund of knowledge or expression, the child in the first few years of his life makes astonishing progress. By the time he is three years old he has learned to understand and speak a difficult language. He knows the names and uses of hundreds of objects about him. He has acquaintance with a considerable number of people, and has learned to adapt himself to their ways. He has gained much information about every phase of his environment which directly touches his life--his mastery of knowledge has grown apace, without rest or pause.

Nor does the development of what we have called *attitudes* lag behind. Parallel with growth in the child's knowledge, his interests are taking root; his ideals are shaping; his standards are developing; his enthusiasms are kindling; his loyalties are being grounded. These changes go on whether we will or not--just because life and growth can not be stopped. The great question that confronts teacher and parent is whether through guidance, that is through education, we shall be able to say *what* attitudes shall arise and *what* motives shall come to rule, rather than to leave this all-important matter to chance or to influence hostile to the child's welfare.

The teacher of religion, like all other teachers, must meet two distinct though related problems in the cultivating of attitudes. These are:

1. The creation of an immediate or direct set of attitudes toward the school and its work. This is needed to motivate effort and insure right impressions.

2. The development of a far-reaching set of attitudes that will
carry out from the classroom into the present and future life of
the pupil. This is needed as a guide and stimulus to spiritual
growth, and as a foundation for character.

ATTITUDES TOWARD THE SCHOOL AND ITS WORK

The older view of education sought to drive the child to effort and secure results through pain and compulsion. It was believed that the pathway to learning must of necessity be dreary and strewn with hardships, if, indeed, not freely watered with the tears of childhood.

Now we know better. A knowledge of child psychology and a more sympathetic insight into child nature have shown us that instead of external compulsion we must get hold of the inner springs of action. No mind can exert its full power unless the driving force comes from *within*. The capacities implanted in the child at his birth do not reach full fruition except when freely and gladly used because their use is a pleasure and satisfaction. If worthy results are to be secured, the *whole self* must be called into action under the stimulus of willingness, desire, and complete assent of the inner self to the tasks imposed. There must be no lagging, nor holding back, nor partial use of powers.

Religious education is, therefore, not simply a question of getting our children into the church schools. That is easy. Parents who themselves do not attend feel that they have more fully done their duty by their children if they send them to the Sunday school. After securing the attendance of the children the great question still remains--that of the *response*, their attitude toward the activities of the school, the completeness with which they give themselves to its work.

A friend who is a State inspector of public schools tells me that the first thing he looks for when he visits a school is the *school spirit*, the attitude of the pupils toward their teachers and the work of the school. If this is good, there is a foundation upon which to build fruitful work; if the spirit is bad, there is no possibility that the work of the school can be up to standard. For it is out of the schoolroom spirit, the classroom attitudes, that the effort necessary to growth and achievement must come.

The spirit of the classroom.--Do the children enjoy the lesson hour? The first of the motivating conditions to seek for our classroom is a prevailing attitude of happiness, good cheer, enjoyment. These are the natural attributes and attitudes of childhood. Unhappiness is an abnormal state for the child. The child's nature unfolds and his mind expands normally only when in an atmosphere of sympathy, kindness, and good feeling. Our pupils must enjoy what they are doing, if they are to give themselves whole-heartedly to it. If loyalty to the school and the church is to result, they must not feel that the Sunday school hour is a drag and a bore. If such is the case, they cannot be expected to carry away lasting impressions for good. They must not look upon attendance as an imposition, nor wait with eager impatience for the closing gong.

While loyalty should be permeated by a sense of duty and obligation, and even of self-sacrifice, it cannot rest on this alone. Most children and youth are loyal to their homes; but this loyalty rests chiefly on a sentiment formed from day to day and year to year out of the satisfying experiences connected with the love, care, protection, and associations of the home. Let these happy, satisfying home experiences be lacking, and loyalty to the home fails or loses its fine quality.

In similar way, if the experiences in the Sunday school and the church continuously yield satisfaction, enjoyment, and good feeling, the child's loyalty and devotion are assured; if, on the other hand, these experiences come to be associated with dislike, reluctance, and aversion, loyalty is in danger of breaking under the strain.

The response of interest.--Are the children interested? While, as we have seen, the atmosphere or spirit of the classroom supplies the condition necessary to successful work, interest supplies the motive force. For interest is the mainspring of action. A child may politely listen, or from a sense of courtesy or good will sit quietly passive and not disturb others, but this does not meet the requirement. His thought, interest, and enthusiasm must be centered on the matter in hand. He must withdraw his attention from all wandering thoughts, passing fancies, distracting surroundings, and concentrate upon the lesson itself. There is no substitute for this.

There is no possibility of making lasting impressions on a mind with its energies dispersed through lack of attention. And there is no possibility of securing fruitful attention without interest.

Interest therefore becomes a primary consideration in our teaching of religion. The teacher must constantly ask himself: "What is the state of my pupils' interest? How completely am I commanding their enthusiasm? Suppose I were to grade them on a scale with *complete-indifference* as the interest zero, and with the *'exploding-point'-of-enthusiasm* as the highest interest mark, where would the score mark of my class stand? And if I cannot reasonably hope to keep my class at the high-water mark of interest at all times, what shall I call an attainable standard? If one hundred per cent is to represent the supreme achievement of interest, shall I be satisfied with fifty per cent, with twenty-five per cent, or with complete indifference? If the minds of my pupils can receive and retain lasting impressions only under the stimulus of the higher range of interest, in how far am I now making lasting impressions on my class? In short, *is the interest attitude of my class as good as I can make it?*"

The sense of victory.--Is there a feeling of confidence and mastery? Do the children *understand* what they are asked to learn? Without this the attitude toward the class hour cannot be good, for the mind is always ill at ease when forced to work upon matter it cannot grasp nor assimilate. Nor is it possible to secure full effort without a reasonable degree of mastery. The feeling of confidence and assurance that comes from successful achievement increases the amount of power available. The victorious army or the winning football team is always more formidable than the same organization when oppressed and disheartened by continued defeat.

If the task is interesting, children do not ask that it shall be easy. Once catch their enthusiasm and they will exert their powers to the full, and take joy in the effort. But the effort must be accompanied by a sense of victory and achievement. There must always be immediately ahead the possibility of winning over the difficulties of their lessons. Except in rare moments of emotional exaltation the most heroic of us are not capable of hurling our best strength against obstacles upon whose resistance we make no impression. And the child possesses almost none of this quality. Without a measurable degree of success in what he attempts to learn his *morale* suffers, enthusiasm fails, and discouragement creeps in to sap his powers.

Kept in the presence of mental tasks he cannot master nor understand, the child will soon lose interest and anticipation in his work. Without mastery intellectual defeat comes to be accepted and expected, and the child forms the fatal habit of submission and giving up. Because he expects defeat from the lesson before him, the learner is already defeated; because he has not learned to look for victory in his study, he will never find it.

Preventing the habit of defeat.--This is all to say that in teaching the child religion we must not constantly confront him with matter that is beyond his grasp and understanding. That we are doing this in some of our lesson systems there can be no doubt. The result is seen in the child's hazy and indefinite ideas about religion; in a later astonishing lack of interest in the problems of religion on the part of adults; in the child's unwillingness to undertake the study of his lessons for the Sunday school; in the fact that to many children the Sunday school lesson hour is a task and a bore; and in the fact that the Sunday school does not in a large degree continue to hold the loyalty of its members after they have reached the age of deciding for themselves whether they will attend. *Fundamental to all successful classroom results with children are enjoyment, interest, and mastery.* How these are to be secured will be developed further as the text proceeds.

ATTITUDES THAT CARRY INTO LIFE BEYOND THE SCHOOL

The great problem of every teacher is to make sure that the effects of his instruction reach beyond the classroom. While the immediate attitudes of the classroom are the first great care, they are but the beginning. Growing out of the work of the church school must be a more permanent set of attitudes that underlie life itself, give foundation to character, and in large degree determine the trend and outcome of achievement. *The cultivation of moral and religious attitudes is probably the most important aim for the Sunday school.* As already explained, the word "attitudes" is used to cover a considerable number of qualities and attributes.

A continuing interest in the Bible and religion.--On the whole, people do not concern themselves about what they are not interested in. They do not read the books, study the pictures, go to hear the speakers, or busy themselves with problems to which their interest does not directly and immediately lead them. A fine sense of duty and obligation is all very well, but it never can take the place of interest as a dynamic force in life.

The number of Bibles sold every year would lead one to suppose that our people are great students of the Scriptures. Yet the almost universal ignorance of the Bible proves that it is one thing to own a Bible, and quite another thing to read it. We may buy the Bible because other people own Bibles, because we believe in its principles, and because it seems altogether desirable to have the Bible among our collection of books. But the extent to which we *read* the Bible depends on our interest in it and the truths with which it deals.

Nor should we forget that, while the United States is rightly counted as one of the great Christian nations, only about two out of five of our people are members of Christian churches. It is true that this proportion would be considerably increased if all churches admitted the younger children to membership; but even making allowance for this fact, it is evident that a great task still confronts the church in interesting our own millions in religion in such a way that they shall take part in its organized activities.

Let each teacher of religion therefore ask himself: "To what extent am I grounding in my pupils a *permanent and continuing interest* in the Bible and in the Christian religion? Growing out of lessons I teach these children are they coming to *like* the Bible? will they want to know more about it? will they turn to it naturally as a matter of course because they have found it interesting and helpful? will they care enough for it through the years to search for its deeper meanings and for its hidden beauties? and because of this will they build the strength and inspiration of the Bible increasingly into their lives?"

And, further: "Are my pupils developing a *growing* interest in religion? Do they increasingly find it attractive and inspiring, or is religion to them chiefly a set of restraints and prohibitions? Do they look upon religion as a means to a happier and fuller life, or as a limitation and check upon life. Is religion being revealed to them as the pearl of great price, or does it possess but little value in their standard of what is worth while?" These questions are of supreme significance, for in their right answers are the very issues of spiritual life for those we teach.

Spiritual responsiveness.--The teacher must accept responsibility for the spiritual growth as well as the intellectual training of his pupils. There is no escape from this. We must be satisfied with nothing less than a constantly increasing consciousness of God's presence and reality in the lives of those we teach.

As the child's knowledge grows and his concept of God, develops, this should naturally and inevitably lead to an increasing warmth of attitude toward God and a tendency to turn to him constantly for guidance, strength, comradeship, and forgiveness. Indeed, the cultivation of this trend of the life toward God is the supreme aim in our religious leadership of children. Without this result, whatever may have been the facts learned or the knowledge gleaned, there has been no worthy progress made in spiritual growth and development.

The evolution of spiritual responsiveness.--The realization of this new spiritual consciousness in the child's life may not involve any special nor abrupt upheaval. If the child is wisely led, and if he develops normally in his religion, it almost certainly will not. Countless thousands of those who are living lives very full of spiritual values have come into the rich consciousness of divine relationship so gradually that the separate steps cannot be distinguished. "First the blade, then the ear, and then the full grain in the ear" is the natural law of spiritual growth.

The bearing of this truth upon our teaching is that we must seek for the unfolding of the child's spiritual nature and for the turning of his thought and affections toward God from the first. We must not point to some distant day ahead when the child will "accept Jesus" or become "a child of God." We must ourselves think of the child, and lead the child to think of himself, as a member of God's family.

This does not mean that the child, as he grows from childhood into youth and adulthood, will not need to make a personal and definite decision to give God and the Christ first place in his life; he will need to do this not once, but many times. It only means that from his earliest years the child is to be made to feel that he belongs to God, and should turn to him as Father and Friend. Day by day and week by week the child should be growing more vitally conscious of God's place in his life, and more responsive to this relationship. Only by this steady and continuous process of growth will the spiritual nature take on the depth and quality which the Christian ideal sets for its attainment.

Ideals and ambitions.--In order that religion may be a helpful reality to the child it must extend to his developing ideals and ambitions. For even children have ideals and ambitions, however crude they may be, or however much they may lack the serious and practical nature they later take on. Probably no child reaches his teens without having many times secretly determined that he would do this or become that, which he has admired in some hero of his own choosing from actual acquaintance or from books or stories. There is no normal child but who has his own notions of greatness and importance, of success and fame, and who wishes and longs for certain things ahead upon which he has set his heart, and which he purposes to attain. The things that he thus values are his ideals, goals to be reached. Ideals are, therefore, guides to action and effort, something to be striven after and sacrificed for. They are the things most worth while, for which we can afford to forego other things of lesser value. It was the force of a great ideal which led Paul to say, "This one thing I do"; and to the attainment of that ideal he gave all his purpose and effort.

To form true ideals requires a trained sense of values; one must develop a power of spiritual perspective, and be able to see things in their true proportions. He must know what things rightly come first if he is to "put first things first;" He must have some training in recognizing the value of "pearls" if he is to see that it is a good exchange to "sell all that he has" in order to "buy the pearl of great price."

This all suggests that one of the responsibilities resting upon us as teachers of religion is to guide the child in the forming of his ideals. We must help him form his notion of what is worthy and admirable in character. We must see that he develops high standards of truth, honesty, obedience, and the other moral virtues which lie at the foundation of all vital religion. We must make certain that his ideals of success and achievement include a large measure of service to his fellows. We must ground him in right personal ideals and standards of purity and clean living. We must make him feel a deep sense of responsibility for the full development and fruitful use of his own powers and abilities. In short, we must with all the wisdom and devotion we possess *bring him to accept the life of Jesus as the ideal and pattern for his own life*.

Fine appreciations.--What one admires is an index to his character. More than this, the quality and tone of one's admirations finally build themselves into his nature and become a part of his very being. Life is infinitely enriched and refined by responding to the beauty, the goodness, and the gladness to be found around us. In Hawthorne's story of The Great Stone Face, the boy Ernest dwelt upon and admired the character revealed in the benignant lines of the great face outlined by the hand of the Creator on the mountainside until the fine qualities which the young boy daily idealized had grown into his own life, and Ernest himself had become the "wise man" whose coming had long been awaited by his people.

It is not enough therefore to learn the *facts* about the lives of the great men and women of the Bible or of other times. The story of their lives must be presented in such a way that *admiration* is compelled from the learner: for only the qualities the child appreciates and admires are finally built into his own ideal. It is not enough that the child shall be taught that God created the world and all that is therein; he must also be brought to appreciate and admire the wonders and beauties of nature as an evidence of God's wisdom, power, and goodness. It is not enough that our pupils shall come to know the chief events in the life of Jesus and the outline of his teachings; they must also find themselves lost in admiration of the matchless qualities of his great personality.

And so also with music, art, architecture, with the fine in human life and conduct, or with great and noble deeds. Inherent in them all are spiritual stimulus and food for the young life, manna upon which the growing soul should feed. But here again the law holds: in order to assimilate them to his life the child *must appreciate, enjoy, admire*. To bring this about is one part of our task as teacher.

Worthy loyalties and devotions.--Every worthy character must have in it a certain power of resistance, a quality that makes it able to withstand hardship for the sake of an ideal or a cause. It is easy enough to be heroic when it costs nothing of effort or sacrifice. There is no trouble in securing supporters for a cause that is popular, or workers when the work called for is interesting and attractive. We are all willing to stand for the right if to stand is agreeable and exhilarating, and does not bring us too much of unpleasantness, pain, or suffering.

But life at its best and noblest does involve some hardship. Much that is best in human experience has come to us through hardship, toil, and suffering cheerfully endured by heroic souls who counted their own lives as naught so that the cause to which they gave themselves might win. The comforts, freedom, and opportunities we enjoy some one paid for, bought with endless effort and sacrifice. Our very religion, the symbol of life, gladness, and salvation, has as its background tragedy, suffering, death, the cross.

The quality that makes us willing to endure and resist for the sake of a cause or an ideal we call *loyalty*. The high value set upon it is seen in the fact that loyalty is the first test of citizenship required; it is a quality admired and praised among all peoples in all relations of life; it is the quality we demand and prize in our friends and associates. On the other hand, disloyalty to country, friends, or trust is universally looked upon as despicable, and punished with contempt, scorn, and hatred.

The appeal to the heroic.--One of the ends of religious teaching is to cultivate in our youth the spirit of loyalty to worthy ideals and causes. Loyalty rests on a stratum of heroism, which is to be found deep down in every normal human being. We must stimulate and appeal to the heroic in the child's nature. We must make him see that the strong and fine men and women are willing to meet much that is hard and disagreeable, so that they may be loyal to their task. We must make him realize that the greatest and most worthy thing one can do is to "endure hardship" for a cause; that to be willing to suffer for an ideal is a mark of strength and courage; and that "having done all to *stand*" is often the best test of character.

Nor must the thought of loyalty be presented to the child only in the abstract. Concrete examples are worth much general explanation and laudation. The loyalties of the great characters of biblical and other times can be made the source of great inspiration; the supreme loyalty of Jesus to his mission will exert a powerful appeal. But loyalty must be made immediate, definite and concrete to the child in his own life; he must not simply admire it afar off. Loyalty must be to him not something to learn about and praise in others, but something he can make use of himself each day without waiting to grow up or become famous. So we will teach the child the loyalties due parents and the home; loyalties to friends and comrades; loyalties to school, community, and country; loyalties to Sunday school, church, and the cause of religion; loyalties to self; loyalties to duty wherever found; and, above all, *loyalties to the Christ and his ideals*.

1. Do your pupils enjoy the church school, and like to come? Do they enjoy the lesson hour? By what means do you tell? Is the spirit of the class good toward the school and toward the class?

How do you judge this?

2. Do your pupils come to the lesson hour full of expectancy? Or is there an indifference and lack of interest with which you have to contend? If the class fails in some degree to manifest expectancy and interest, where do you judge the trouble to lie? What is the remedy?

3. To what degree do you think your pupils are comprehending and mastering what you are teaching them? How does their mastery compare with that secured in the public schools? Have you plans for making their mastery more complete?

4. Do you judge that your pupils are developing such an attitude toward the Bible that their interest will carry on beyond the time they are in your class? Do you think they have an increasing interest in religion? Are you making these questions one of the problems of your teaching?

5. Are your pupils developing through the work you are doing a growing consciousness of God in their lives? Do they count themselves as children of God? Just what do you believe is the status of your children spiritually? Do they need conservation or conversion? What difference will your answer make in your teaching?

6. To what degree are your pupils loyal to the church school? To their particular class? To the church? What are the tests of loyalty? Do they come regularly? Do they seek to promote the interests of the class and the school? Do they do their part? What can be done to increase loyalty?

FOR FURTHER READING
Wilber, A Child's Religion.
Bushnell, Christian Nurture (Revised Ed.).
Betts, The Mind and Its Education, chapter on "Interest."
Fisk, Boy Life and Self-Government.

CHAPTER VI
CONNECTING RELIGIOUS INSTRUCTION WITH LIFE AND CONDUCT

We have now come to the third of the great trio of aims in religious education--right living. This, of course, is *the* aim to which the gathering of religious knowledge and the setting up of religious attitudes are but secondary; or, rather, fruitful religious knowledge, and right religious attitudes are the *means* by which to lead to skill in right living as the *end*.

In the last analysis the child does not come to us that he may learn this or that set of facts, nor that he may develop such and such a group of feelings, but that through these he may live better. The final test of our teaching, therefore, is just this: Because of our instruction, does the child *live* differently here and now, as a child, in all his multiform relations in the home, the school, the church, the community, and in his own personal life? Are the lessons we teach translated continuously into better conduct, finer acts, and stronger character as shown in the daily run of the learner's experience?

It is true that the full fruits of our teaching and of the child's learning must wait for time and experience to bring the individual to fuller development. But it is also true that it is impossible for the child to lay up a store of unused knowledge and have it remain against a later time of need in a distant future. The only knowledge that forms a vital part of our equipment is knowledge that is in active service, guiding our thought and decisions from day to day. Unused knowledge quickly vanishes away, leaving little more permanent impression on the life than that left on the wave when we plunge our hand into the water and take it out again. In similar way the interests, ideals, and emotions which are aroused without at the same time affording a natural outlet for expression in deeds and conduct soon fade away without having fulfilled the purpose for which they exist. The great thing in religious education is to find *immediate and natural outlet in expression*, a way for the child to *use* what he learns; to get the child to *do* those things pointed out by the lessons we teach him.

Religion drawing closer to life.--This is the only method of religious education that will meet the requirements of these times upon the Christian religion. The unmistakable trend of modern Christianity is to connect religion more closely and vitally with life itself--to make it a *mode of living* in a deeper sense than has obtained since the days of Christ upon earth. This is a very hopeful sign, for it accords completely with the spirit and message of Jesus. When he said, "By their fruit ye shall know them," what did he mean but that the quality and value of a man's religion is to be known by its outcome in, deeds and action? When he said, "Not everyone that saith. Lord! Lord! but he that doeth..."; and again, "He that heareth these sayings of mine and doeth them...," was he not again emphasizing the great; truth that one's religion is tested only by the extent to which it is tied up with his daily living?

The teacher will, therefore, say to himself, The religious knowledge I am putting into the minds of my pupils is of supreme importance--if it makes them live better and act more nobly; the religious attitudes and emotions I am cultivating in my class are full of value and significance--if they cause their possessors to live more broadly, sympathetically, usefully, and happily. The true teacher will then add, And it is my task *to see that this result follows without fail!*

RELIGIOUS HABITS AS AN AIM

Indirectly all this is to say that our first care in teaching the young child religion should be to lead him to form *religious habits*. For our lives are controlled by a great network of habits which come to us as the result of acts often repeated, until they have become as second nature. There are many things about the child's religion that should become second nature; that is, should become habit--and which are not certain and secure until they have grown into habits. For example, it is wholly desirable to have the habit of attending church, of personal devotions, and of resisting temptation, so well fixed that the acts required for each take care of themselves with a minimum of struggle and decision each time the occasion arises. Not only will this method require less strain and compulsion on our part, but it will result in more uniform churchgoing, attention to devotions, and the overcoming of temptation.

The age for habit forming.--The principle, then, is simple and clear. At the beginning of the child's contact with the church school he cannot grasp the broader and deeper meanings of religion; but he can during this period be led into the doing of right acts and deeds, and thus have his religious habits started. At a time when his brain is yet unripe, and hence unready for the more difficult truths or the more exalted emotions of religion, the child is at his best in the matter of habit-forming. For habits grounded in early childhood are more easily formed and more deeply imbedded than those acquired at any later time, and they exert a stronger control over the life.

How habits grow.--But habits do not come of their own accord; they must be gradually acquired. Immediately back of every habit lies a chain of acts out of which the habit grows. Given the acts, and the habit is as sure to follow as night the day. Hence the great thing in religious instruction of the young is to afford opportunity for our teaching to be carried as immediately as may be over into deeds.

As we make the desired impressions upon the minds of our pupils, we must see that the way is reasonably open for *expression*. The lessons should be so direct, simple, and clear that there is no difficulty in connecting them immediately with the daily life, and then we should do our best to see *that the connection is made*.

As we teach we should have in mind the week that lies ahead in the child's life--in the home, the school, on the playground, in the community, and in whatever personal situations and problems we may know are being met. Then we should use every power as a teacher to make sure that we help the child meet the challenge of his daily life with the finest acts, best deeds, and noblest conduct possible for him to command.

APPLICATION OF RELIGIOUS INSTRUCTION TO THE DAILY LIFE

One great purpose, then, in religious instruction is to attach the stimulus and appeal of religion to the common round of daily life and experience of the child. As Christ came that we might have life, not a future life alone, but a full, happy, and worthy life in the present as well, so we come to the child as a teacher to help him in his *life* here and now. Our task at this point is to lead him to practice the great fundamental virtues whose value has been proved through ages of human experience, to incorporate directly into his living the lessons learned slowly and with great sacrifice by generations which have preceded him. Our aim will be to lead our pupils, out of their own choice and conviction, to adopt and follow a *code of action* such as the following:

I will respect and care for my body. I will keep my body clean and pure. I will try to avoid sickness and disease. I will breathe good air day and night, and live out of doors all I can. Because I shall need all my strength and endurance at their best, I will pay no toll to the poisons of alcohol and nicotine. I will be temperate in my food, and eat such foods as will favor growth, health, and strength. I will bathe often, play and work hard, and get plenty of sleep and rest. My character will be judged by my poise and carriage; therefore I will try to walk, stand, and sit well, and not allow my manner to show slouchiness and carelessness. Both because of my own self-respect and because I owe it to others, I will strive to make myself neat and attractive in dress and person. I will treat my body right so far as I can know what is best for it, and will do nothing to defile or injure any part of it. I will try to keep my body a fit dwelling place for my soul, for God gave them both to me. And I will do all I can to make my home, school, and community a beautiful and healthful place for others to live.

I will keep good-natured, cheerful, and responsive. Tasks grow easier and loads lighter when one is cheerful. I will therefore guard against gloomy and sullen moods, which not only make me unhappy, but cause unhappiness to those about me. I will watch that I may not be cross and irritable at home, and shall do my part to make home the bright and happy place I wish it to be. I will be careful not to grumble nor whine when things go wrong, or when I cannot have my own way. I will remember that troubles flee when we refuse to think about them. I will refuse to give way to ill temper, for I would not become its slave; rather will I learn to laugh at small troubles and annoyances that cannot be cured. If I am feeling sad or unhappy, I will stop to speak a kind word or do a fine deed, and the gloom will disappear.

I will take pride in work and thrift. The world has no place for the one who shirks. Some one toiled for every comfort I enjoy; some one worked for the clothing, shelter, food, and all the other good things that come to me. I must do my part, work, help others, and especially help in the home. I will not slight my tasks, but say; "I can!" and go at my work with a will. What though the task be hard--if it is mine, I'll do it! What though the lesson be long--if it is to be learned, I'll master it! If I can stand at the head of my class, I will, but only when I have earned the right by honest effort. Because the world contains so many who must go hungry for want of food, and who lack other necessities and comforts, I will not needlessly spend nor waste anything of value. I will take pride in thrift and saving, and do all I can to encourage this spirit in others. I will respect and honor all worthy toil. I will thank the good God every day that he allows me to take part in the work round about me, and ask him to help me to do my share well in each seen or unseen part of every task.

I will be honest and speak the truth. Only one who is honest is worthy of trust, and he who tells a lie confesses that he is a coward and afraid to let the truth be known. I will be honest even in little things, and will have no "white lies." Though it may seem a trifle to cheat in school or not play fair in a game, I will be above all trickery and deceit. Both in play and in work my fight must be clean and fair; I shall ask but for an even chance. I will give full value for whatever I receive; if I work for wages, I must make sure to earn them; if I secure honors or grades at school, I must win them. I will let alone all games of chance, for gambling takes what one has not earned, and is therefore stealing.

I will be obedient to the rules of my home and school and to the laws of my country. The rules of home and school and the laws of state and nation are made for the good of all; and wherever freedom rules there laws must be obeyed. I will not quibble nor seek to evade, but give prompt and cheerful obedience wherever my duty is to obey. I will honor the law and respect those in authority over me. I will not be one of those who must needs be watched, and narrowly held to right paths. I will obey not because of fear or compulsion, but gladly, because I choose to do the right. I will not tempt others to disobedience, nor to the violation of the law. I will be a loyal member of my home and school and a patriotic citizen of my country, doing all in my power to advance their welfare and interests.

I will be courteous and kind. The men and women whom people love and admire are courteous and kind. The strong and the brave are never cruel, they do not willingly injure others nor hurt their feelings. I will strive each day to be courteous at home, kind to those who are nearest to me, and helpful to my friends and companions. I will not knowingly cause pain or suffering to any person. I will extend my protection and kindness to all animals and every dumb and helpless thing, remembering that pain is pain wherever felt, in a worm as well as in a man. Especially will I show my best courtesy to aged and infirm persons, and to all such as may need help. It will be my high privilege to render service to any who are unfortunate, crippled, or in distress, I will do unto others what I would have them do unto me.

I will show courage and self-control. I should not want to be a coward, for cowardice always brings pity and contempt. I know that all must at times meet pain and suffering; and when the time comes to me I must not lose my courage and self-control; I will not shrink nor cringe, but find strength in remembering that many have suffered and endured without complaint. I will avoid danger and unnecessary risk whenever possible, but if accident or duty puts me in a place of danger, I must try to keep a cool head and to show my mettle by doing my full duty bravely. When sometimes things go wrong, and I cannot have my own way, I shall show my courage and self-command by keeping my temper and tongue under control; I will be a good sportsman and not complain, nag, nor find fault. I will make it a rule, if I feel my anger rising, to think twice before I speak or act. If I have wronged or offended anyone, I will be strong enough to go and make it right, confessing my fault. When I am tempted to think or do or say what I know to be wrong, I will ask my heavenly Father for strength to overcome the temptation. It will be my constant purpose and care to keep myself pure in thought, word, and deed.

I will be dependable and do my duty. The world needs men and women on whom it can depend, and who are not afraid to do their duty at whatever cost. I must learn to face hardship and to meet the disagreeable without giving way before it. I must not ask what road is easy, but what way is right--and then do my duty. When I know I **ought** I must be able to say **I will**, even if the choice brings me pain and trouble. If I have undertaken any trust or task, I must not lag nor weaken nor grow careless, but faithfully see it through to the end. When my country calls, or the world needs my services, I must not consult my own wishes or convenience, but unfalteringly follow where duty leads. Whenever I can with justice and self-respect, I will avoid a quarrel; but I will not sit idly by and see injustice and oppression brought on the weak and helpless if I can prevent.

I will love and enjoy nature. The birds, the flowers, the trees and the brooks make the best of friends. I will study the great book of nature around me, and seek to learn the secrets of its many forms. I will live as much as I can in the great out-of-doors, finding in its beauty and freshness new evidences of God's wisdom and goodness. I will never injure nor destroy, but do all I can to protect the beautiful living and growing things about me. I will find joy in the storm, the rain, and the snow, and then no day will seem dreary or dull to me. I will seek for some good purpose in all harmless created things, making comrades of my animal playmates, and taking an interest in all such things as creep or crawl or fly; and need then never be lonely nor lack good company. I will look upon the glory of the sunset, the wonder of a starlit night, the sparkle of the dew, and then reverently thank God that he has made the great world so beautiful and good.

I will each day turn to my heavenly Father for help, strength, and forgiveness. I know I cannot live my life as I should live it without God's help and counsel. I will therefore turn to him in prayer that he will guide me when I am puzzled or uncertain, that he will give me victory when I am tempted to do wrong, that he will give me courage when I falter or am afraid, that he will forgive me when I have sinned or failed in my duty. I will take for my standard of life and action the example of Jesus, and show my love and appreciation by living as fully as I can the kind of life he lived. I know that I cannot have God's presence in my life unless I keep my heart pure and my conduct right; I will therefore, with his help, as nearly as I can, live from day to day as I think God would have me live, I will take time morning and evening of each day for a few moments of prayer, quiet thought, and for the study of the Bible. I will do my best to be a worthy Christian.

*   *   *   *   *

The teacher, of course, will need to adapt the application of such principles as those we have been discussing to the age and the needs of his pupils. Such lessons cannot be presented as so much abstract truth. The purpose, as we have already seen, is to lead the child to make such high ideals his habit of life and action, so that at last they may govern his conduct and become an inseparable part of his character. To do this, such ideals must be made desirable and attainable.

PARTICIPATION IN THE WORK OF THE CHURCH AND SOCIAL SERVICE

The forming of religious social habits is as important as the forming of religious personal habits. From his earliest years the child should come to look on his church, his Sunday school, and the class to which he belongs as a responsibility in which he has a personal share. His experience in connection with these organizations should be so interesting and satisfying that his attendance does not have to be compelled, but so that his loyalty, affection, and pride naturally lead him to them.

When this is accomplished, the basis of good attendance is secured, and the foundation laid for later participation in all forms of church work. Once the right spirit is created and right habits developed, unpleasant weather, bad roads or streets, getting up late on Sunday mornings, nor any other obstacles will stand in the way of regular church and Sunday school attendance any more than of day-school attendance. And until the church has its children (and their homes) so trained that attendance on the church school is regular throughout the year, our instruction must of necessity fail to reach its full aim.

Learning to take responsibility for others.--One of the greatest lessons a child can learn from his lessons in religion is that he is his brother's keeper. The instincts of childhood are naturally selfish and self-centered; the sense of responsibility for others must be gradually trained and developed. A double purpose can therefore be served by enlisting the children of our classes as recruiting officers to secure new members, and to look up any who may have dropped out or whose attendance is irregular. The sense of pride and emulation in such work, and the feeling on the part of our pupils that they are actually accomplishing something definite for their class or school will do much to cement loyalty and train the children to assume responsibility for their comrades.

This ***pride of the group*** is a strong force during later childhood and adolescence, and can be fruitfully used in religious training. The boy or the girl Scout takes great pride in doing acts of kindness and service without personal reward, just ***because that is one of the things that scouting stands for***. "Scouts are expected to do this," or "Scouts are not expected to do that," has all the force of law to the loyal Scout.

The Sunday school class can command the same spirit if the proper appeal is made. In its neighborhood work and on many special occasions the church and the Sunday school will have need of messenger service. Errands will have to be run, articles will have to be gathered and distributed, calls will have to be made, funds will have to be collected, and a hundred other things done which children can do as well or better than anyone else. And it is precisely in these practical acts of homely service that the child gets his best training in the social side of religion.

Laboratory work in religion. The wise teacher will therefore seize upon every opportunity to find something worth while for his pupils ***to do***. He will have them help with the distribution of supplies in the classroom; he will see that they volunteer to help the super-intendent or other officials who may need assistance; he will give them responsibility in decorating the church or classroom for special occasions; he will leave to their cooperation as large a measure as possible of the work to be done in arranging and carrying out class or school picnics, excursions, social gatherings, and the like; he will arrange for special groups to visit the aged, sick, or shut-in for the purpose of singing gospel songs, and will open the way for those who are qualified to do so to read the Bible or other matter to the blind or those whose sight is failing. In short, the devoted teacher who understands the laws of childhood will make his instruction as nearly as possible a ***laboratory course*** in religion, finding the material and the occasion in the human needs and the opportunities for loving service which lie closest at hand.

Assuming personal responsibility.--The sense of the child's responsibility for his class and school must also carry into the exercise of the school itself. The boy should be led to prepare his lesson because of the truth it contains; but also because a recitation cannot be a success unless the pupils know their lesson and do their part. He should pay his share toward the running of the school and church because it is our duty to give, but also because he feels a personal responsibility for his church and his class. He should take part in public prayer or the leadership of meetings, when asked to do, because it is right and proper to do these things, but also because he realizes that each member of the class and school owes it to the organization to do his share.

Nothing can take the place of whole-hearted, joyous participation in the real activities of the Sunday school as a means of catching the interest of the members and securing their loyalty; for interest and loyalty finally attach to those activities in which we have a share. The school in which the child finds a chance to **express** the lessons and **put into practice** the maxims he is taught is the school which is building Christian character and providing for future religious leadership.

Participation in singing.--Especially should we develop in our children the ability and will to engage in religious singing. Almost every child can sing, and all children respond to the appeal of music adapted to their understanding. The most expert and inspiring leadership which the church can command should be placed in charge of the children's singing in the Sunday school.

If it comes to the question of selecting between a director for the adult choir and a soloist for the general congregation on the one hand, or an efficient organizer and director of children's music on the other hand, there should not be a moment's hesitation on the part of any church to supply the needs of the children first. The aim should then be to have **all** the children sing, and allow none to form the habit of depending on the older members or on a few leaders to supply the singing for the entire school. Those who possess special ability in music should be formed into choruses, orchestras, school bands, or similar organizations. Not only will all this add to the interest and effectiveness of the school itself, but, not less important, will be helping to **form the music habit** in connection with sacred music.

Training in giving.--The missionary enterprises of the church afford one of the best opportunities for giving the child practical training in the social aspect of religion. It is not enough that the children shall be told the stories of the missionary heroes and given the picture of the needs of the people in far-away lands. Once the imagination is stirred and the emotions wanned by this instruction, an immediate and natural outlet in expression must be found if these lessons are to fulfill their end.

Children should early be led into giving money for missionary purposes, and this as far as possible should be their *own* money which they themselves have earned. For the child to go to his father on a Sunday morning for money for the missionary collection does not answer the need on the educational side; it is the child's real *sharing* that leaves the impression and teaches the lesson.

There is also real educational value in leading children to give clothing, food, or other necessities for the use of the needy. Here, again, the giving should involve something of real sacrifice and sharing, and not consist merely in giving away that for which the child himself no longer cares. The joint giving by a class or the entire school for the support of a missionary worker whose name is known, and a somewhat detailed report of whose work is received, lends immediateness and reality to the participation of the pupils. A strong appeal can be made to the spirit of giving by the adoption by the class of some needy boy or girl whose Christian education is provided for by the efforts of the class, and to whom personal letters can be written and from whom replies may be received.

Social service.--The children of our Sunday schools should be given an active and prominent part in all forms of community welfare service. The successful enlistment of the Boy Scouts and the Girl Scouts in many valuable forms of community enterprises contains a vital suggestion and lesson for the church school. Wherever good deeds need to be done, wherever help needs to be rendered, wherever kindness and service are necessary, there the children should be called upon to do their part. If the tasks and responsibilities are suited to the various ages, there will be no trouble about securing response. Nor, on the other hand, will there be any doubt but that the lessons learned will be entirely vital and will serve to connect the religious motive with everyday life and its activities.

Religion finding expression in the home.--No system or method of religious instruction is effective the results of which do not find expression in the life of the home. It is here in the intimate relations of children with each other and with their parents that the moral and religious lessons of forbearance, good will, and mutual service find most frequent and vital opportunity for application.

Children need early to be made to see their individual and joint responsibility for the happiness, cheerfulness, good nature, and general social tone of their home; and to help at these points should become a part of their religion. They should be stimulated to share in the care of the home, and not to shirk their part of its work. They should be interested in the home's finances, and come to feel a personal responsibility for saving or earning as the situation may require. They should have a definite part in the hospitality which the home extends to its friends and neighbors, and come by experience to sense the true meaning of the word "neighborliness."

The appearance and attractiveness of their home should be a matter of pride with children, and this feeling should cause them to be careful in their own habits of neatness, cleanliness, and order about the home. All these things have a bearing on the foundations of character and are therefore a legitimate concern in religious instruction.

The final tests of our instruction.--In such things as we have been discussing, then, we find one of the surest tests of the outcome of our teaching the child religion--Are the lessons carrying over? Is the child, because of our contact with him, growing in attractiveness and strength of personality and character? Is he developing a habit of prayer, devotion, spiritual turning to God? Is he doing a reasonable amount of reading and study of the Bible and the lesson material of the school? Is he taking such personal part in the various social and religious activities of the church and the community that he is "getting his hand in," and developing the attachments and loyalties which can come only through participation? In short, is the child given a chance to apply, and does he daily put into practice and thus into character, the content and spirit of what we teach him?

The answers we must return to these questions will measure our success as teachers and determine the value coming to the child from our instruction.

    1. To what extent do you believe your pupils are living differently in their daily lives for the instruction you are giving them? Do you definitely plan your teaching to accomplish this aim? For example, what *definite* results are you seeking from the next lesson?

2. Can you think your class over pupil by pupil and decide which of these points in the *code of action* most needs be stressed in individual cases? Do the topics in this code suggest points of emphasis which might serve for many different lessons? Is there danger of loss in efficiency if we try to stress too many of the points at one time?

3. Are the children of your class interested in keeping up the membership and attendance? What specific part and responsibility do you give the members in this matter? Is it possible that you could plan to use their help more fully and effectively?

4. Suppose you try making a list of all the different lines of participation in religious activities directly opened up to the pupils of your class by the church and the church school. Is the list as long as it should be? What further provision could be made for the children to have definite responsibility and activity?

5. Do you think that your pupils are becoming increasingly inclined to look upon religion as a *mode of living?* For example, will your children be more agreeable, responsive, obedient, and helpful in the home next week for the lessons you have been teaching them? Will they have higher standards of conduct in the school and on the playground?

FOR FURTHER READING
Dewey, Moral Principles in Education.
Sharp, Education for Character.
Partridge, Genetic Philosophy of Education, chapters on "Moral and Religious Education."
Mumford, The Dawn of Character.
Richardson, The Religious Education of Adolescents.
Alexander, Boy Training.

CHAPTER VII
THE SUBJECT MATTER OF RELIGIOUS EDUCATION

We have seen in an earlier chapter how the subject matter of religious education must be selected in accordance with the *aims* we would have it accomplish in the lives of our pupils. We have also considered in separate chapters the religious *knowledge* required, the religious *attitudes* demanded and the practical *applications* of religious instruction to be made or the *expression* to be sought in the everyday life. Let us now examine somewhat more completely the particular phases of subject matter which should be used to attain these ends--To what sources shall we go for the material for the religious instruction of our children? What subject matter shall we put into the curriculum of religious education? This is a question of supreme importance to the individual, to the church, and to civilization.

SOURCES OF MATERIAL

First of all we must realize that the sources of religious material are almost infinitely broad and rich. They are much broader than the Bible. I would not be misunderstood on this point. I conceive the Bible as the matchless textbook of religion, the great repository of spiritual wisdom through the ages. It is the primary source to which we must go for material for religious instruction, not just because it is the Bible, but because its truths are the surest guide ever formulated for spiritual development.

Yet human experience and human problems are broader than the Bible. New ages bring new conditions and new needs. Eternal truths may take on new forms to meet new problems. God inspired the writers of his Word, but he also inspires other writers, whose works are not included in the canon. He echoed in the voice of Isaiah and Jeremiah, but he also touches with the flame of eloquence other lips than those of the prophets. He spoke to the child Samuel, but he also speaks to-day to every heart that will hear his voice. He flamed from the burning bush for Moses, but in like manner he shines from every glowing sunset for those whose eyes can there behold his glory.

Breadth and richness of religious material.--The sources of material available for the religious education of childhood are therefore as broad as the multiform ways in which God speaks to men, and as rich as all the great experiences of men which have left their impress upon civilization. Besides the beautiful story of God creating the earth, we have the wonderful miracle of constant re-creation going on before our eyes in the succession of generations of all living things.

Besides the deathless accounts of the heroism of such men as Elijah, Daniel, and Paul, we have the immortal deeds of Livingstone, Taylor, and Luther. Besides the womanly courage and strength of Esther and Ruth, we have the matchless devotion of Florence Nightingale, Frances Willard, Alice Freeman Palmer, and Jane Addams. Besides the stirring poetry of the Bible, and its appealing stories, myths and parables, we have the marvelous treasure house of religious literary wealth found in the writings of Tennyson, Whittier, Bryant, Phillips Brooks, and many other writers.

Material to be drawn from many sources.--The material for religious teaching lying ready to our hand is measureless in amount, and must be wisely chosen. In addition to material from the Bible, which always must be the center and foundation of the religious curriculum, should be taken other material from nature; from biography, history, and life itself; from literature and story; from science and the great world of objects about us; from music, and from art. All of this multiform subject matter must be welded together with a common purpose, and so permeated with the religious motive and application that it will touch the child's spiritual thought and feeling at many points of his experience.

At no moment, however, must we forget that our primary purpose is not simply to teach the child stories, literature, history, or science, but *religion*. By the proper use of this broader field of material religion may be given a new and more practical significance, and the Bible itself take on a deeper meaning from finding its setting among realities closely related to the child's daily life.

MATERIAL FROM THE BIBLE

The very nature of the Bible requires that we make the most careful selections from it in choosing the material for religious instruction of children. Not all parts of the Bible are of equal value as educational material, and some parts of it have no place in the course of study before full mental development has been reached.

How we came by the Bible.--It will help us to understand and apply these principles if we remember how we came by the Bible. First of all is the fact that the Bible grew out of religion and the life of the church, and not religion and the church out of the Bible. The Bible is not one book, as many think of it, but a collection of sixty-six books, which happen to be bound together. In fact, all sixty-six of these books are now printed and bound separately by the American Bible Society, and sold at a penny each. These sixty-six books were centuries in the making, and they came from widely separated regions. Different ones of them were originally written in different tongues--Hebrew, Greek, and Aramaic.

The earlier Christians had, of course, only the scriptures of the Old Testament. It was nearly four hundred years after Christ had lived on earth before we had a list of the New Testament books such as our Bible now contains. In the middle of the second century only about half of the present New Testament was in use as a part of the Scriptures. Some of the books which we now include were at one time or another omitted by the Christian scholars, and several books were at one time accorded a place which are not now accepted as a part of the Bible. The authorship of a considerable number of the books of the Bible is unknown, and even the exact period to which they belong is uncertain.

The different writers wrote with different purposes--one was a historian; another a poet; another, as Paul, a theologian; another a preacher; another a teller of stories and myths, or a user of parables. Paul wrote his letters to local churches or to individuals, to answer immediate questions or meet definite conditions and needs.

Jesus left no written word, so far as we know, and the first written accounts we have of his life and work were begun forty or fifty years after his death.

The problem of selecting Bible material adapted to children.--The Bible was therefore a slow growth. It did not take its form in accordance with any particular or definite plan. It never was meant as a connected, organized textbook, to be studied in the same serial and continuous order as other books. It was not written originally for children, but for adults to read.

Its enduring quality proves that the writers of the Bible lived close to the heart and thought of God, and were therefore inspired of him. But we can grant this and still feel free to select from its lessons and truths the ones that are most directly fitted to meet the needs of our children as we train them in religion. We can love and prize the Bible for all that it means and has meant to the world, and yet treat it as a *means* and not an *end* in itself. We can believe in its truth and inspiration, and still leave out of the lessons we give our children the sections which contain little of interest or significance for the child's life, or matter which is beyond his grasp and understanding.

Material which may be omitted.--This point of view implies the omission, at least from the earlier part of the child's religious education, of much material from different parts of the Bible; these irrelevant sections or material not suited to the understanding of childhood may remain for adult study.

For example, we may leave out such matter as the following: The detailed account of the old Hebrew law as given in Leviticus; much of the Hebrew history which has no direct bearing on the understanding of their religion; details of the institution of the passover, and other ecclesiastical arrangements; the philosophy of the book of Job; genealogies which have no especial significance nor interest; the succession of judges and kings; dates and chronological sequences of no particular importance; any stories or matter clearly meant to be understood as allegory or myth, but which the child would misunderstand, or take as literal and so get a mistaken point of view which later would have to be corrected; the theology of Paul as set forth in his letters; matter which shows a lower state of morality than that on which we live; and *such other matter as does not have some direct and discoverable relation to the religious knowledge, attitudes, and applications which should result from the study*.

After all such material of doubtful value to the child has been omitted, there still remains an abundance of rich, inspiring, and helpful subject matter.

The principle on which to select material from the Bible is clear: Know what the child *is ready for* in his grasp and understanding; know *what he needs* to stimulate his religious imagination and feeling and further his moral and religious development. Then choose the material accordingly.

Bible material for earlier childhood.--For the period of *earlier childhood* (ages three or four to eight or nine) we shall need to omit all such material as deals with the broader and deeper theory of religion. This is not the time to teach the child the significance of the atonement, the mystery of regeneration, the power of faith, nor the doctrine of the Trinity. Those sections of the Bible which deal with such far-reaching concepts as these must wait for later age and fuller development.

The child is now ready to understand about God as the Creator of the earth and of man; he is ready to comprehend God as Father and Friend, and Jesus as Brother and Helper; he is ready to learn lessons of obedience to God, and of being sorry when he has done wrong; he is therefore ready to understand forgiveness; he is ready to learn all lessons of kindliness, truthfulness, and honesty, and of courage; he is ready to learn to pray, and to thank God for his care and kindliness. The Bible material taught the child should therefore center upon these things. The simple, beautiful story of the creation; stories of God's love, provision, and protection and of Christ's care for children; incidents of heroic obedience and of God's punishment of disobedience; stories of forgiveness following wrongdoing and repentance; stories of courage and strength under temptation to do wrong; lessons upon prayer and praise and thanksgiving--this is the kind of material from the Bible which we should give our children of this younger age.

The greater part of the material for this stage of instruction will come from the Old Testament, and will make the child familiar with the childhood of Moses, Samuel, Joseph, David, and other such characters as possess an especial appeal to the child's sympathy and imagination. The New Testament must be drawn upon for the material bearing upon the birth and childhood of Jesus.

Material for later childhood.--In the period of *later childhood* (ages eight or nine to twelve or thirteen) the child is still unready for the more difficult and doctrinal parts of the Scriptures. Most of the impulses of earlier childhood still continue, even if in modified form. Types of Bible material adapted to the earlier years, therefore, still can be used to advantage.

A marked characteristic of this period, however, is the tendency to hero worship and to be influenced by the ideals found in those who are loved and admired. This is the time, therefore, to bring to the child the splendid example and inspiration of the great Bible characters. The life and work of Moses, the story of Joseph and his triumph over discouragements and difficulties, the stern integrity and courage of Elijah and the other prophets, the beautiful stories of Ruth, Esther, Miriam, and Rachel, but above all the story of Jesus--the account of these lives will minister to the child's impulse to hero worship and at the same time teach him some of the most valuable lessons in religion.

During later childhood, the sense of personal responsibility for conduct is developing, and the comprehension of the meaning of wrongdoing and sin. This is the time, therefore, to bring in lessons from the Bible showing the results of sin and disobedience to God, and the necessity for repentance and prayer for forgiveness. During this period also, while the social interests are not yet at their highest, the narrow selfishness of earlier childhood should be giving way to a more generous and social attitude, and a sense of responsibility for the welfare and happiness of others.

To meet the needs of the growing nature at this point many lessons should be provided containing suggestions and inspiration from high examples of self-forgetfulness, sacrifice, and service as found in the life of Jesus, Paul, and many others from the Old and the New Testament. The child's growing acquaintance with the world about him and his study of nature in the day schools prepare him for still further deepening his realization of God beneficently at work in the material universe. Abundant material may be found in the Bible to deepen and strengthen the learner's love and appreciation of the beautiful and good in the physical world.

Material for adolescence.--The ***adolescent*** period (ages twelve or thirteen to twenty or twenty-two) is the transition stage from childhood to maturity. The broader, deeper, and more permanent interests are now developing, and character is taking its permanent trend. Conduct, choice, and decision are becoming more personal and less dependent on others. A new sense of self is developing, and deeper recognition of individual responsibility is growing.

It is all-important that at this time the Bible material should furnish the most of inspiration and guidance possible. The life and service of Jesus will now exert its fullest appeal, and should be studied in detail. The work and service of Paul and of the apostles in founding the early church will fire the imagination and quicken the sense of the world's need of great lives. The ethical teachings of the Bible should now be made prominent, and should be made effective in shaping the ideals of personal and of social conduct which are crystallizing. The development of the Hebrew religion, with its ethical teaching, and the moral quality of the Christian religion are now fruitful matter for study.

During the later part of adolescence the youth is ready to consider biblical matter that throws light on the deeper meaning of sin, of redemption, of repentance, of forgiveness, of regeneration, and other such vital concepts from our religion. The simplest and least controversial interpretations--that is, the broader and more significant meanings--should be presented, and not the overspeculative and disputed interpretations, which are almost certain to lead to mental and perhaps spiritual disturbance and even doubt.

The guiding principle.--For whatever age or stage of the child's development we are responsible, we will follow the same principle. Because we want to cultivate in the child a deep and continuing interest in the Bible and the things for which it stands, we will seek always to bring to him such material as will appeal to his interest, stir his imagination, and quicken his sense of spiritual values. Since we desire to influence the learner's deeds and shape his conduct through our teaching, we will present to him those lessons from the Bible which are most naturally and inevitably translated into daily living. First we will know what impression we seek to make or what application we hope to secure, and then wisely choose from the rich Bible sources the material which will most surely accomplish this end.

STORY MATERIAL

The story is the chief and most effective means of teaching the younger child religion, nor does the appeal of the story form of expressing truth lose its charm for those of older years. Lessons incomprehensible if put into formal precept can be readily understood by the child if made a part of life and action, and the story does just this. It shows virtue being lived; goodness proving itself; strength, courage, and gentleness expressing themselves in practice; and selfishness, ugliness, and wrong revealing their unlovely quality. Taught in the story way, the lesson is so plain that even the child cannot miss it.

The story also appeals to the child's imagination, which is so ready for use and so vivid, and which it is so necessary to employ upon good material in order to safeguard its possessor from using it in harmful ways. Long before the child has come to the age of understanding reasoned truth, therefore, he may well have implanted in his mind many of the deepest and most beautiful religious truths which will ever come to him.

The Old Testament rich in story material.--The wonderful religious and ethical teachings of the Old Testament belong to a child-nation, and were written by men who were in freshness of heart and in picturesqueness and simplicity of thought essentially child-men; hence these teachings are in large part written in the form of story, of legend, of allegory, of myth, of vivid picture and of unrimed poetry. It is this quality which makes the material so suitable to the child. The deeper meanings of the story do not have to be explained, even to the young child; he grasps them, not all at once, but slowly and surely as the story is told and retold to him. If the story is properly told, the child does not have to be taught that the Bible myth or legend *is* myth or legend; he accepts it as such, not troubling to analyze or explain, but unconsciously appropriating such inner meaning as his experience makes possible, and building the lesson into the structure of his growing nature.

If full advantage is taken of the story as a means of religious teaching, the grounding of the child in the fundamental concepts and attitudes of religion can be accomplished with certainty and effectiveness almost before the age for really formal instruction has come.

The ethical quality alone not enough in stories.--Many stories of highest religious value are available from other sources than the Bible, yet no other stories can ever wholly take the place of the Bible stories. For the Bible stories possess one essential quality lacking in stories from other sources; the Bible stories *are saturated with God*. And this is an element wholly vital to the child's instruction in religion.

We cannot teach the child religion on the basis of ethics alone, necessary as morality is to life. We cannot help the child to spiritual growth and the consciousness of God in his life without having the matter we teach him permeated and made alive with the spirit and presence of God in it. Nor is there the least difficulty for the child to understand God in the stories. The child, like the Hebrews themselves, does not feel any necessity of explaining or accounting for God, but readily and naturally accepts him and the part he plays in our affairs as a matter of course.

Stories from other than Bible sources.--But once a sufficient proportion of Bible stories is provided for, stories should be freely drawn from other fields. An abundance of rich material possessing true religious worth can be found in the myths, legends, folk lore, and heroic tales of many literatures. These are a treasure house with which every teacher of children should be familiar; nor is the task a burdensome one, for much of this material holds a value and charm even for the older ones of us.

Later writers have enriched the fund of material available for children by treating many of the aspects of nature in story form, thereby opening up to the mind and heart of the child something of the meaning and beauty of the physical world, and showing God as the giver of many good gifts in this realm of our lives. There are also available the stories of history, and of the real men and women whose lives have blessed our own or other times, and whose deeds and achievements will appeal to the imagination and stir the ideals of youth.

The teacher as a story teller.--The successful teacher of religion must therefore possess the art which will enable him to use the story as one of the chief forms of material in his instruction. He must *know* the stories. He must be able to tell them interestingly. The story loses half of its effectiveness if it must be *read* to the child, but it may lose in similar proportion if it is haltingly or ineffectively told. It is not necessary, at least for the younger children, to use a large number of stories. In fact, there is positive disadvantage in attempting to employ so many stories that the child does not become wholly familiar with each separate one. Children do not tire of the stories they like; indeed, their love for a story increases as they come to know it well, and they will demand to have the same story told over and over in preference to a new one.

The use of the story with older children.--A mistake has been made in not a few of the Sunday school lesson series in sharply reducing the story material for all ages above the primary grades. It must be remembered that while the older child has more power to grasp and understand abstract lessons than the younger child, there is no age or stage of development at which the story and the concrete illustration are not an attractive and effective mode of teaching. Surely, all through the junior and intermediate grades the story should be one of the chief forms of material for religious instruction, while for adolescents stories will still be far from negligible.

The principles of story-using, then, are clear in the teaching of religion: ***Make the story one of the chief instruments of instruction; see that it is charged with religious and moral value; make sure it is adapted to the age of the learner, and that it is well told; for younger children use few stories frequently repeated until they are well known; do not insist that the child shall at first grasp the deeper meanings of the story, make sure of interest and enjoyment, and the meaning will come later.***

MATERIAL FROM NATURE

The child's spontaneous love of nature and ready response to the world of objects about him open up rich sources of material for religious instruction. God who creates the beautiful flowers, who causes the breezes to blow, who carpets the earth with green, who paints the autumn hillside with glowing color, who directs the coming and going of the seasons, who tells the buds when to swell and the leaves to unfold, who directs the sparrow in its flight and the bee in its search, who is in the song of the birds and the whisper of the leaves, who sends his rain and makes the thunder roll--this God can be brought, through the medium of nature's forms, very near to the child. And the love and appreciation which the child lavishes on the dear and beautiful things about him will extend naturally and without trouble of comprehension to their Creator.

Nature material useful for all ages.--Most of the lesson material now supplied for our Sunday schools use a considerable amount of nature material in the earlier grades, but some important lesson series omit most or all nature material from the junior department on. This is a serious mistake. All through childhood and youth the pupil is continuing in the public school his study of nature and its laws. Along with this broadening of knowledge of the natural world should be the deepening of appreciation of its spiritual meaning, and the inspiration to praise and worship which comes from it. One does not, or at least should not, at any age outgrow his response to the wonders and beauties which nature unfolds before him who has eyes to see its inner meaning. None can afford to lose the simple, untutored awe with which children and primitive men look out upon the world.

Carlyle, recognizing this truth, exclaims: "This green, flowery, rock-built earth, the trees, the mountains, rivers, many-sounding seas; that great deep sea of azure that swims overhead; the winds sweeping through it; the black cloud fashioning itself together, now pouring out fire, now hail and rain; what *is* it? Aye, what?... An unspeakable, godlike thing, toward which the best attitude for us, after never so much science, is awe, devout prostration, and humility of soul; worship, if not in words, then in silence."

In the same spirit Max Mueller exhorts us: "Look at the dawn, and forget for a moment your astronomy; and I ask you whether, when the dark veil of night is slowly lifted, and the air becomes transparent and alive, and light streams forth you know not whence, you would not feel that your eye were looking into the very eye of the Infinite?" And Emerson reminds us: "If the stars should appear one night in a thousand years, how would men believe and adore; and preserve for many generations the remembrance of the city of God which had been shown! But every night come out these envoys of beauty, and light the universe with their admonishing smile."

When, then, shall we have become too far removed from childhood to be beyond the appeal of nature to our souls? When shall we cease to "hold communion with her visible forms," and to find in them one of the many avenues which God has left open for us to use in approaching him! What teacher of us will dare to leave out of his instruction at any stage of the child's development the beneficent and wonder-working God of nature as he smiles his benediction upon us from the myriad common things around us!

MATERIAL FROM HISTORY AND BIOGRAPHY

God is to be found in the lives of nations and of men not less than in nature, and the evidences and effects of his presence there should be taught our children. The spirit which Jesus revealed in his life upon earth is exemplified in the lives of many of his followers who joyously spend themselves in the service of others. Men who set the standard for manliness, and women whose character and lives are the best definition of womanliness, are as much a revelation of God's work and power as a constellation of stars or the bloom of the rose.

The example of great lives.--So, along with the great Bible characters we will bring to the child the men, and women of other generations. We will bring to him the great souls who, as missionaries, have carried the Light to those who sit in darkness; those who in honesty and integrity of purpose have served as leaders of nations or armies or movements to the blessing of humanity; those who, with the love of God in their hearts, have gone out as ministers, teachers, writers of books, singers of songs, makers of pictures, healers of sickness; or those who, in any field, of toil or service, have given the cup of cold water in the name of the Master.

And we will bring to the child the story of the nations, showing him one people growing in strength, power, and happiness while following God's plan of human justice, mercy, and kindness; and another going down to destruction, its very name and speech forgotten, because it became arrogant and perverse and forgot the ways of righteousness. At the proper time in their development we will bring to our pupils the life and problems of the present--the wrongs that need to be righted, the causes that need to be defended and carried through to victory, the evil that needs to be suppressed, the work of Christ and the church which is, awaiting workers. Thus shall we seek to bring the challenge of life itself to those we teach.

PICTURE MATERIAL

No discussion of the curriculum can ignore the use of *pictures* as teaching material. Teachers of religion have long recognized the value of visual instruction, and every lesson series now has its full quota of picture cards and other forms of pictorial material.

In this picture material may roughly be distinguished three great types: (1) the *symbolical* picture; (2) the rather *formal* picture, often badly conceived and executed, always dealing with biblical characters or incidents; and (3) the more universalized type drawn from every field of pictorial art, representing not only biblical personages and events, but also typifying aesthetic and moral values of every range adapted to the understanding and appreciation of the child.

Types of pictures.--Representative of the first, or symbolical, pictorial type are found the more or less crude pen drawings of such things as the *heart* with a key, an open *Bible with a torch* beside it, tombstone-like drawings representing the *Tables of the Law* or three *interlocking circles representing the Trinity, etc.*

Not only are all these abstract concepts beyond the grasp or need of the child at the age when the pictures are represented, but the symbols are in no degree suggestive to the child of the lesson intended; they are devoid of meaning, without interest, possess no artistic value, and lack all teaching significance. Such material should be discarded, and better pictures provided.

The second type of pictures, or those dealing with Bible topics, contain teaching power, but should be merged with the third, or true art, type. That is to say, biblical subjects, moral lessons, and inspiring ideals should be treated by *true artists* and made a part of the religious curriculum for childhood. Wherever suitable masterpieces executed by great artists can be found, copies should be made available for teaching religion. Hundreds of such pictures hang in our art galleries, and not a few of them have already been incorporated into several excellent series for the Sunday school.

Further, the pictures offered children should be as carefully selected with reference to *what they are to teach*, and should be as carefully graded to meet the age, interests, and appreciations of the child as are other forms of curriculum material. Some otherwise excellent picture sets of recent publication lose the greater part of their usefulness as teaching helps through the lack of this adaptation.

MUSIC IN THE CURRICULUM

Music as a part of the curriculum of religious education offers a peculiarly difficult problem. No other form of expression can take the place of music in creating a spirit of reverence and devotion, or in inducing an attitude of worship and inspiring religious feeling and emotion. Children ought to sing much both in the church school and in their worship at home.

Yet most of our hymns have been written for adults, and most of the music is better adapted to adult singing than to the singing of children. The ragtime hymns which find a place in many Sunday school exercises need only to be mentioned to be condemned. On the other hand, many of the finest hymns of the church are beyond the grasp of the child in sentiment and beyond his ability in music. The church seriously needs a revival of religious hymnology for children. In the meantime the greatest care should be used to select hymns for children's singing which possess as fully as may be three requisites: (1) music adapted to the child's capacity, (2) music that is worthy, interesting and devotional, and (3) words within the child's understanding and interest, and suitable in sentiment.

1. Many persons think that teaching the child religion and teaching him the Bible are precisely the same thing. Do you think it is possible to teach the child parts of the Bible without securing for him spiritual development from the process? Is it possible to make the Bible itself mean more to the child by supplementing it with material from other sources?

2. Do you ever find lessons provided for your class which are not adapted to their age and understanding? If so, do you feel free to supplement or substitute with material which meets their needs? Do you have sufficient command of the material of the Bible and other sources so that you can do this successfully?

3. Do you know a considerable number of stories adapted to the age of your pupils? Are you constantly adding to your list? Are you a good story teller? Are you studying to improve in this line? Even if your lesson material does not provide stories, do you bring such material in for your class?

4. What use do you make of nature in the teaching of religion? President Hall thinks that nature material is one of the best sources of religious instruction. Do you agree with him? Are you sufficiently in love with nature yourself, and sufficiently acquainted with nature so that you can successfully use the nature motive in your teaching?

5. Do you constantly make use of stories and illustrations from the lives of great men and women in your teaching? Do you take a reasonable proportion of these from contemporary life? Do you bring in stories of fine actions by boys and girls? What use have you been making of events in the lives of nations in your teaching? Are you reading and studying to become more fully prepared to use this type of material?

FOR FURTHER READING
Houghton, Telling Bible Stories.
Raymont, The Use of the Bible in the Education of the Young.
Brace, The Training of the Twelve.
Drake, Problems of Religion, chapter IX.
Athearn, The Church School.

CHAPTER VIII
THE ORGANIZATION OF MATERIAL

The organization of material to adapt it to the learner's mind and arrange it for the teacher's use in instruction is hardly less important than choosing the subject matter itself. By organization is meant the plan, order, or arrangement by which the different sections of material are made ready for presentation to the child. The problems of organization may apply either (1) to the *curriculum as a whole*, or (2) to any particular section of it used for *a day's lesson*.

It is possible to distinguish four different types of organization commonly used in preparing material for religious instruction:

1. The *haphazard*, in which there is no definite plan or order, no thread of purpose or relationship uniting the parts, no guiding principle determining the order and sequence.

2. The *logical*, in which the nature and relationships of the material itself determine the plan and order, the question of ease and effectiveness in learning being secondary or not considered.

3. The *chronological*, applicable especially to historical material, in which the events, characters, and facts are taken up in the order of the time of their appearance and their sequence in the entire situation or account.

4. The *psychological*, in which the first and most important question is the most natural and favorable mode of approach for the learner--how the material shall be planned and arranged to suit his power and grasp, appeal to his interest, and relate itself to his actual needs and experience.

TYPES OF ORGANIZATION

Haphazard organization.--The *haphazard* plan, which is really no plan at all, is, of course, wholly indefensible. No teacher has a right to go before his class with his material in so nebulous a state that it lacks coordination and purpose. It is this that results in chance and unrelated questions, irrelevant discussions, and fruitless wanderings without definite purpose over the field of the lesson, such as may sometimes be seen in church classes.

The outcome of such instruction hardly can be more than occasional, disconnected scraps of information, or fragmentary impressions which are never gathered up and bound together into completed ideals and convictions. The haphazard type of organization may result from incompetence, indifference, and failure to prepare, or from taking a ready-made and poorly prepared plan from the "lesson helps" which is not adapted to our class. Pity the child assigned to a class presided over by a teacher who esteems his privilege so lightly as not to make ready for his task by careful planning.

Logical organization.--In the *logical* arrangement of material, the first care is not given to planning it in the most favorable way for the one who studies and learns it, but, rather, to fit together the different parts of the subject matter in the way best suited to its logical relationships. The child is pedagogically ignored; the material receives primary consideration. The logical order of material fits the mind of the adult, the scholar, the expert, the master in his field of knowledge; it begins with the most general and abstract truths. But the child naturally starts with the particular and the concrete. It gives rules, principles, definitions, while the child asks for illustrations, applications, real instances, and actual cases.

The logical method is adapted to the trained explorer in the fields of learning, to one who has been over the ground and knows all of its details, and not to the young novice just starting his discoveries in regions that are strange to him. The logical plan will teach the young child the general plan of salvation, man's fall and need of redemption, the wonder and significance of the atonement, and gracious effects of divine regeneration working in the heart--all of which he needs finally to know--but *not as a child just beginning the study of religion*. The child must arrive at the general plan of salvation through realizing the saving power at work in his own life; he must come to understand the fall of man and his need of redemption through meeting his own childhood temptations and through seeing the effects of sin at work around him; he must understand the atonement and regeneration through the present and growing consciousness of a living Christ daily strengthening and redeeming his life.

Chronological organization.--The *chronological* order of material is desirable at the later stages of the child's growth and development. But in earlier years the time sequence is not the chief consideration. This is because the child's historical sense is not yet ready for the concept of cause and effect at work to produce certain inevitable results in the lives of men or nations.

The sequence in which certain kings reigned, or the order in which certain events took place, or in which certain books of the Bible were written is not the important thing for early childhood. At this time the great object is to seize upon the event, the character or the incident, and make it real *and vital*; it is to bring the meaning of the lesson out of its past setting and attach it to the child's immediate present.

Psychological organization.--It is the *psychological* organization of material that should obtain both in the curriculum as a whole and in the planning of the individual lessons. We must not think, however, that a psychological order of material necessarily makes it illogical. On the other hand, the arrangement of material that takes into account the child's needs is certain to make it more logical *to him* than any adult scheme or plan could do. That is most logical to any person which most completely fits into his particular system of thought and understanding. If we succeed in making our plan of presenting material to the child wholly psychological, therefore, we need not be concerned; all other questions of organization will take care of themselves, and *the psychological will constantly tend to become logical*.

What is meant by a psychological method of arranging material for presentation has already been discussed (Chapter III). Suffice it to say here that it is simply *planning the subject matter to fit the mind and needs of the child*--arranging for the easiest and most natural mode of approach, securing the most immediate points of contact for interest and application, remembering all the time that the child speaks as a child, thinks as a child, understands as a child.

Jesus' use of the psychological plan.--The teacher who seeks to master the spirit of the psychological presentation of religious material should study the teaching-method of Jesus. Always he came close to the life and experience of those he would impress; always he proceeds from the plane of the learner's experiences, under-standing, and interests. Did he want to teach a great lesson about the different ways in which men receive truth into their lives?--"Behold a sower went forth to sow." Did he seek to explain the stupendous meaning and significance of the new kingdom of the spirit which he came to reveal?--"The kingdom of heaven is like to a grain of mustard seed," or, "The kingdom of heaven is like unto leaven, which a woman took and hid in three measures of meal," or, "The kingdom of heaven is likened unto a man which sowed good seed in his field."

And with this simple, direct, psychological, homely mode of approach to great themes Jesus made his hearers understand vital lessons, and at the same time showed them how to apply the lessons to their own lives. So throughout all his teaching and preaching; the lesson of the talents, the prodigal son, the workers in the vineyard, the wedding feast, placing a little child in the midst of them--all these and many other concrete points of departure illustrate the highest degree of skill in the psychological use of material.

ORGANIZATION OF THE CURRICULUM AS A WHOLE

The material offered in the curriculum of our church schools is not, taking it in all its parts, as well organized as that in our public day schools. This is in part because the material of religion is somewhat more difficult to grade and arrange for the child than the material of arithmetic, geography, and other school subjects. But it is also because the church school has not fully kept pace with the progress in education of recent times.

A century or two ago the day-school texts were not well graded and adapted to children; now, we have carefully graded systems of texts in all school subjects.

While the logical and the chronological method of organization still holds a place in many of the public school texts, the psychological point of view, which considers the needs of the child first, is characteristic of all the better schoolbooks of the present. Just because religion is more difficult to teach than grammar or history or arithmetic, we should plan with all the insight and skill at our command to prepare the religious material for our children so that its arrangement will not suffer by comparison with day-school material.

Three types of lesson material.--Material representing three different types of organization and content of curriculum material is now available and being used in our church schools:

1. The *Uniform Lessons*, which are ungraded, and which give (with few minor exceptions) the same topics and material to all ages of pupils from the youngest children to adults.

2. The *Graded Lessons*, which seek to adapt the topics and subject matter to the age and needs of the child, and which therefore present different material for the various grades or divisions of the school. These are usually printed in leaflet or pamphlet form.

3. Real *textbooks of religion* which are based on the principles used in making day-school texts. The material is divided into chapters, each dealing with some theme or topic adapted to the age of the child, the lessons not being dated nor arranged to cover a certain cycle of subject matter as in the case of the regular lesson series. The books are printed and bound much the same as day-school texts.

The uniform lessons.--Although many churches still employ the *Uniform Lessons*, we shall not hesitate to say that no church school is justified in this day of educational enlightenment in using a system of ungraded lessons. Such lessons are planned for adults. They ignore the needs of the child, and force upon him material for which he is in no sense ready, while at the same time omitting matter that he needs and is capable of understanding and using. For example, some of the topics which primary children, juniors, and all alike find in their ungraded lessons of current date are, *man's fall*, the *atonement*, *regeneration*, the *city of God*, *faith*--splendid topics all, but too strong meat for babes.

Why should we thus ignore the educational progress of the age, starve our children spiritually, and hamper them in their religious development by this obsolete system of education which has been long since outgrown in the public schools? Why should we not ignore tradition, prejudice, and personal preference, where these are in the way, and *let the needs of the child decide*? Why should thousands of church schools to-day be using the Uniform Lessons?

Some use them because they are cheaper; others because they always have used them and do not like the trouble and disarrangement of a change; others because of the doubtful theory of the inspiration that comes from having all the members of the family studying the same lesson at the same time (we do not expect all the family to read or study the same material in other lines); and perhaps others because they have not been accustomed to thinking of religious education following the same principles and laws as other education. But whatever the explanation of the use of the Uniform Lessons in our church schools in the past, let us now see to it that they give way to better material. Let us not be satisfied, even, when the ungraded uniform lessons are "improved"; they should not be improved, but discarded.

Graded lessons.--A large and increasing number of our best church schools are now using some form of graded lesson material based on the topics supplied by the International Lesson Committee. Each great denomination has its own lesson writers, who take these topics and elaborate them into the graded lessons such as we know in the Berean Series, the Keystone Series, the Pilgrim Series, the Westminster Series, etc. All such lesson material, which seeks to adapt the material to the needs of the child as he progresses year by year from infancy to adulthood, is infinitely superior to any form of ungraded material. It is easier and more interesting for the child to learn, less difficult for the teacher to present; and its value in guiding spiritual development immeasurably greater.

Some form of closely *graded lessons* is the only kind of material which should be used in our church schools; the children have the same need and the same right to material graded and prepared to meet their understanding in religion as in language or in science. But when we employ graded lessons we must make sure that *the child, and not the subject matter; is the basis of the grading*. We must make certain that the writer of the lessons knows the mental grasp, the type of interests, the characteristic attitudes, and the social activities of the child at the different stages, and then arranges the material to meet these needs. We must not simply aim to cover so much biblical material, even if we select it as well as we may to come within the child's grasp; we must have his real religious needs, his religious growth, and his spiritual development in mind, and provide for these.

Adapting graded lessons to young children.--In the graded series of lessons now most commonly used in the church schools the material is, on the whole, fairly well selected to meet the needs of the **beginners** and the **primary section**. Interesting stories are told, and much nature material presented. The work is, of course, all presented to the pupils by the teacher, as the children cannot yet read. In some cases the stories used are undoubtedly too difficult, and not a few of them lack the elements of good story-telling.

Yet the instruction usually centers about the topics most needed by the child at this time--the love and care of God both for our lives and in the world of nature about us; the Christ-child and his care for children; lessons of kindness, obedience and love in the home, etc. Because of this directness of appeal the child responds to the material and the teacher finds her task much easier and more fruitful than with the difficult topics of the ungraded lessons.

Graded lessons not all well adapted to ages.--As the graded lessons pass on into the **junior** age, the adaptation of material is generally less successful than for the primary grades. The topics are based less on the interests and spiritual needs of the child, and more on the material. The lessons for the greater part consist of biblical material only, and are often too difficult for the child to be interested in them or to understand them. No coordinating principle relates the topics to each other, and the material consequently comes to the child in rather disconnected scraps. Too frequently this material, because it belongs to a later stage of development, is without any particular or direct bearing on the learner's experience, and hence not assimilated into his life.

The remedy here is to use a larger proportion of story material, of biography, of lessons from nature, and of such gems of literature as carry a spiritual message suited to the child. The caution is to avoid over-intellectualizing the child's religious instruction, and to make sure that we do not outrun his rate of development in the material we give him. The same principles should carry over into the intermediate, or preadolescence, age. The hero-worship stage is then, at hand, and the lesson material should be arranged to meet the natural demand of the child for action and adventure.

In planning a graded series of lessons it is not less important to meet the needs of the *seniors*, or adolescents, than of the younger pupils. This has not always been accomplished. Here again, as in the earlier years, the immediate interests and needs of the learner are to be the key to the planning of material. A series of unrelated topics dealing with a distant time and civilization, with little or no application to the problems and interests that are now thronging upon the youth, will make small appeal to him. The youth's growing consciousness of social problems, his interest in a vocation, his increasing feeling of personal responsibility as a member of the family, the community, the church and the brotherhood of men are suggestions of the nature of the topics that should now form the foundation of religious study and instruction.

It is possible that the forgetting of this simple fact in the planning of material for adolescent pupils is one chief reason for the tragic loss of interest in the Sunday school which so often occurs at the adolescent stage.

Text books of religious material.--The ***text book*** type of religious material differs more in the organization and arrangement of material than in the subject matter itself. The lessons are not based on a set cycle of biblical material, though, of course, such material is freely used. Usually one topic or theme is followed throughout the text, the number of lessons or chapters provided being intended for one year's work. The following titles of texts now in use suggest the nature of the subject matter: "God's Wonder World," "Heroes of Israel," "Heroic Lives," "The Story of Jesus," "The Making of a Nation," "Our Part in the World," "The Story of a Book," "The Manhood of the Master," "Problems of Boyhood," "Social Duties," "The Testing of a Nation's Ideals."

Beyond question, the material we teach our children in religion should be organized and published as real ***books*** and not as paper-covered or unbound serial pamphlets. There is really no more reason why we should divide religious material up into lessons to be dated, and issued month by month, than why we should thus divide and issue material in geography, history, reading, or any other school subject. Children who are accustomed in day schools to well-made, well-bound books, with good paper and clear, readable print, cannot be expected to respond favorably to the ordinary lesson pamphlet. The child should be encouraged and helped in the building of his own library of religious books, but this can hardly be done as long as his church-school material comes to him in temporary form, much of it less attractive on the mechanical side than the average advertising leaflet which so freely finds its unread way to the waste basket.

Many of the Sunday school leaflets carry at the top (or the bottom) of the page an advertisement of the denominational lesson series--matter in which the child is not concerned, which injures the appearance of the page, and which lowers the dignity and value of the publication. And some lesson pamphlets are even disfigured with commercial advertisements, sometimes of articles of doubtful value, and always with the effect of lowering the tone of the subject matter to which it is attached. Religious material printed in worthy book form escapes these indignities. That textbooks in religion will cost more than the present cheap form of material is possible. But what matter! We are willing to supply our children with the texts needed in their day-school work; shall we not supply them with the books required for their training in religion? If the texts prove too much of a financial burden for the children or their parents, there is no reason why the church should not follow the example of the public school district and itself own the books, lending them for free use to the pupils.

Guiding principles.--The principles for the organization of the church-school curriculum, are, then, clear. Its lessons should start with matter adapted to the youngest child. It should present a continuous series of steps providing material of broadening scope adapted to each age or stage from childhood to full maturity. Its order and arrangement should at all times be decided by the needs and development of the learner, and should make constant point of contact with his life and experience. It should be printed in attractive textbook form, the paper, type, illustrations, and binding being equal to the best standards prevailing in public-school texts. In short, we should apply the same scientific and educational knowledge, and the same business ability in preparing and issuing our religious material that we devote to this phase of general education.

ORGANIZING THE DAILY LESSON MATERIAL

The teacher's plan or organization of each lesson for presentation to the class in the recitation is a matter of supreme importance. Even the best and most experienced teachers never reach the point where they do not need to prepare specifically for each recitation. No matter how complete the knowledge of the subject, nor how often one has taught it, there is always the necessity of fitting it directly to the needs and interests of the particular class before us. This preparation should result in a definitely worked out *lesson plan* which, though it may finally be modified to fit situations as they arise in the class discussion, will nevertheless serve as an outline of procedure for the recitation. Even the teachers' manual supplied with most of the lesson series cannot take the place of this definite, individual plan prepared by the teacher himself for his immediate class.

The lesson plan.--The first step in arranging a lesson plan is to determine the range and amount of material which is to be presented to accomplish the aim of the class hour. This will include the lesson or story from the Bible, nature material, memory work, music, pictures or any other subject matter to be considered. In determining this point the age of the children, the time available, and the nature of the subject must all be taken into account. It is a mistake to attempt more than can be done well, or to try to do so many things that the recitation is too much hurried to be interesting or profitable.

The lesson plan should provide for a few chief points or topics, with the smaller points and the illustrations grouped under these. To have many topics receiving the same amount of emphasis in a lesson indicates poor organization. For example, in teaching the lesson of *obedience* from the Garden of Eden story the material may well be grouped under the following topics: 1. The many good and beautiful things God had given Adam and Eve, 2. There was one thing only which they might not have. 3. Their disobedience in desiring and taking this one thing, 4. Their feeling of guilt and unhappiness which made them hide from God. Under these four general heads will come all the stories, illustrations, and applications necessary to make the lesson very real to children.

Small matters of large import.--Of course the particular questions to be asked and the more immediate applications to be made must await the unfolding of the lesson discussion with the class. Good planning requires, however, that we have a set of pivotal questions thought out and set down for our guidance; and also suggestions for illustrations and applications under the various topics. If expression work is to be used, this should be noted in its proper place, and provision made for carrying it out. In planning for older classes, reference should be made in the plan to special assignments to be made in books, magazines or any other material.

Provision should be made in the plan for a summary at the end of the lesson period, and for the making of the final impression which the class are to carry away with them. Nor must the assignment of the next lesson be forgotten. Probably no small proportion of the characteristic failure of pupils to prepare their lessons comes from lack of definite assignments showing the child just what he is expected to do, and how to do it.

Details of a typical lesson plan.--Let us suppose that we are to teach the lesson of obedience from the story of Adam and Eve to children of early primary age. Our *Lesson Plan* might be something as follows:

I. *The Aim or Purpose of the Lesson*--OBEDIENCE.
  1. Knowledge or information to be given the class--
a. Of the Bible story itself.
b. Of the fact that God requires obedience.
c. That disobedience brings sorrow and punishment.
d. That children owe obedience to parents and teachers.
  2. Attitudes, and feeling response to be sought.
a. Interest in and liking for the Bible story.
b. Appreciation of God's many gifts to his children.
c. Desire to please God with obedience.
d. Sorrow for acts of disobedience.
e. Respect for authority of home, school and law.
  3. Applications to the child's life and conduct.
a. Acts of obedience to God in being kind, cheerful, and helpful to others.

b. Cheerful obedience in home and school with no lagging nor ill nature.

c. Prayer for forgiveness for any act of disobedience.

II. *Material or Subject Matter to be Presented.*

1. The story of Adam and Eve in the Garden.

The version of the story is important. The original from the Bible is too difficult. If the lesson material does not offer the story in satisfactory form, go to one of the many books of Bible stories and find a rendering suited to your class. Be able to tell the story well.

2. Pictures of Adam and Eve in the Garden.

Be sure the picture is interesting, well executed, and that it shows attractive and beautiful things.

3. Prayer on obedience.

The prayer to be brief and simple, asking God to help each one to obey him and to obey father and mother, and to forgive us when we do not obey.

4. Music.

If possible, the music may correlate with the thought of the lesson. If not, let it be devotional and adapted to the children in words and melody.

5. Handwork or other form of expression material.

Cutting and pasting pictures in notebooks; coloring, or other such work, to be done either in the classroom or at home.

III. *Mode of Procedure--the Presentation, or Instruction.*

1. Greetings to the class--opening prayer and song.

2. Introduction of the lesson and telling of the story.

3. Discussion, questions and illustrations to reveal:

a. The many beautiful gifts which God had given Adam and Eve, and which he gives us.

b. How Adam and Eve were allowed to have everything except just one thing among many. Application of this thought to child's life at home, etc.

c. How Adam and Eve yielded to temptation and disobeyed. Practical application to child's life.

d. How Adam and Eve felt ashamed and guilty after they had disobeyed God, and how they tried to hide from him. This can be made very real to children.

e. How punishment follows disobedience.

f. Why we must ask for forgiveness when we have been disobedient.

4. Summary, or brief restatement of chief impressions to carry away, and of applications to be made in the week ahead by the children themselves.

5. Closing prayer and song.

Adapting the lesson plan to its uses.--It is, of course, evident that lesson plans can be made of all degrees of complexity and completeness. With a little practice the teacher can easily decide the kind of plan that best suits himself and his particular grade of work. On the one hand, the plan should not be so detailed as to become burdensome to follow in the lesson hour. On the other hand, it should not be so brief and sketchy as not to bring out the significant elements of the lesson.

Different grades of pupils and different subjects will require different lesson plans. It is probable, however, that the three major heads of "Aims," "Material," and "Mode of Procedure" will prove serviceable in all plan making. While the teacher should have his *plan book* at hand in the recitation, he must not become its slave, nor allow its use to kill spontaneity and responsiveness in his teaching. Both the subject matter and the day's plan should be so well mastered that no more than an occasional glance at the details in the plan book will be required. Nothing must be allowed to come between the teacher's best personality and his class.

1. Have you heard lectures, sermons, or lessons which were constructed after the haphazard plan? Were they easy to follow and

to remember? Did they develop a line of thought in a successful way? Do you think that the haphazard type of organization indicates either lack of preparation or lack of ability?

2. Do you definitely try to organize your daily lesson material on a psychological plan? How can you tell whether you have succeeded? Are you close enough to the minds and hearts of your pupils so that you are able to judge quite accurately the best mode of approach in planning a lesson?

3. Do you study the lesson helps provided with your lesson material? Do you find them helpful? If you find that they are not well adapted to your particular class, have you the ability to make the suggestions over to fit your class?

4. Do you make a reasonably complete and wholly definite lesson plan for each lesson? Do you keep a plan book, so that you may be able to look back at any time and see just what devices you have used? If you have not done this, will you not start the practice now?

5. What type of lesson material do you use, uniform, graded, or textbook? Are you acquainted with other series or material for the same grades? Would it not be worth your while to secure supplemental material of such kinds?

6. Do you read a journal of Sunday school method dealing with problems of your grade of teaching? If day-school teachers find it worth while to read professional journals, do not church-school teachers need their help as much? If you do not know what journals to secure, your pastor can advise you.

FOR FURTHER READING
Strayer, A Brief Course in the Teaching Process, chapter XVI.
Betts, Class Room Method and Management, chapter VIII.
Earhart, Types of Teaching.

CHAPTER IX
THE TECHNIQUE OF TEACHING

Our teaching must be made to stick. None but lasting impressions possess permanent value. The sermons, the lectures, the lessons that we remember and later dwell upon are the ones that finally are built into our lives and that shape our thinking and acting. Impressions that touch only the outer surfaces of the mind are no more lasting than writing traced on the sand. Truths that are but dimly felt or but partially grasped soon fade away, leaving little more effect than the shadows which are thrown on the picture screen.

Especially do these facts hold for the teacher in the church-school class. For the impressions made in the church-school lesson hour bear a larger proportion to the entire result than in the public school. This is because of the nature of the subject we teach, and also because of the fact that most of our pupils come to the class with little or no previous study on the lesson material. This leaves them almost completely dependent on the recitation itself for the actual results of their church-school attendance. The responsibility thus placed upon the teacher is correspondingly great, and requires unusual devotion and skill.

ATTENTION TO KEY

The things that impress us, the things that we remember and apply, are the things to which we have attended wholly and completely. The mind may be thought of as a stream of energy. There is only so much volume, so much force that can be brought to bear upon the work in hand. In attention the mind's energy is piled up in a "wave" on the problem occupying our thought, and results follow as they cannot if the stream of mental energy flows at a dead level from lack of concentration.

Or, again, the mind's energy may be likened to the energy of sunlight as it falls in a flood through the window upon our desk. This diffuse sunlight will brighten the desk top and slightly increase its temperature, but no striking effects are seen. But now take this same amount of sun energy and, passing it through a lens, focus it on a small spot on the desk top--and the wood bursts almost at once into flame. What *diffuse* energy coming from the sun could never do, *concentrated* energy easily and quickly accomplished. Attention is to the mind's energy what the lens is to the sun's energy. It gathers the mental power into a focus on the lesson to be learned or the truth to be mastered, and the concentrated energy of the mind readily accomplishes results that would be impossible with the mental energy scattered or not directed to the one thing under consideration. The teacher's first and most persistent problem in the recitation is, therefore, to gain and hold the highest possible degree of attention.

Three types of appeal to attention.--We are told that there are three kinds of attention, though this is not strictly true. There is really only one *kind* of attention, for attention is but the *concentration of the mind's energy on one object or thought*. What is meant is that there are three different *ways of securing* or appealing to attention. Each type of attention is named in accordance with the kind of compulsion or appeal necessary to command it, as follows:

1. *Involuntary* attention, or attention that is demanded of us by some sudden or startling stimulus, as the stroke of a bell, the whistle of a train, an aching tooth, the teacher rapping on the desk with a ruler.

2. *Nonvoluntary*, or spontaneous, attention that we give easily and naturally, with no effort of self-compulsion. This kind of attention is compelled by *interest*, and, when left unhindered, will be guided by the nature of our interest.

3. *Voluntary* attention, or attention that is compelled by effort and power of will, and thereby required to concern itself with some particular object of thought when the mind's pull or desire is in another direction.

How each type of attention works.--The first of these types of attention, the *involuntary*, has so little place in education that we shall not need to discuss it here. The teacher who raps the desk, or taps the bell to secure attention which should come from interest must remember that in such case the attention is given to the *stimulus*, that is, to the signal, and not to the lesson, and this very fact makes all such efforts to secure attention a distraction in themselves.

The *spontaneous*, or nonvoluntary, attention that arises from interest is the basis on which all true education and training must be founded. The mind, and especially the child's mind, is so constituted that its full power is not brought to bear except under the stimulus and compulsion of interest. It is the story which is so entrancing that we cannot tear ourself away from it, the game which is so exciting as to cause us to forget all else in watching it, the lecture or sermon which is so interesting that we are absorbed in listening to it, that claims our best thought and comprehension. It is when our mind's powers are thus driven by a tidal wave of interest that we are at our best, and that we receive and register the lasting impressions which become a part of our mental equipment and character.

This does not mean, however, that there is no place for *voluntary* attention in the child's training. For not everything can be made so inviting that the appeal will at all times bring about the concentration necessary. And in any case a part of the child's education is to learn self-direction, self-compulsion, and self-control. There are many occasions when the interest is not sufficient to hold attention steady to the task in hand; it is at this point that voluntary attention should come in to add its help to provide the required effort and concentration. There are many circumstances under which interest will secure a moderate amount of application of mental energy to the task, but where the will should step in and command an additional supply of effort, and so attain full instead of partial results.

Children should, therefore, be trained to *give* attention. They should be taught to take and maintain the attitude of attention throughout the lesson period, and not be allowed to become listless or troublesome the moment their interest is not held to the highest pitch.

THE APPEAL TO INTEREST

Sometimes we speak of "arousing the child's interest," or of "creating an interest" in a topic we are teaching. Strictly speaking, this is incorrect. The child's interest, when rightly appealed to, does not have to be "aroused," nor does interest have to be "created."

Every normal child is naturally alert, curious, ***interested*** in what concerns him. Who has not taken a child for a walk or gone with a group of children on an excursion, and been amazed at their capacity for interest in every object about them and for attention to an endless chain of impressions from their varied environment? Who has not observed children in a game, and noted their complete absorption in its changing aspects? Who has not called a child from an interesting tale in a book he was reading, and found that it required the combined force of our authority and the child's will to break the spell of his interest and separate him from his book? Interest is always ready to flow in resistless current if we can but find the right channel and a way to set it free. When we find our class uninterested, therefore, we must first of all seek the explanation not in the children, but in ourselves, our methods, or the matter we teach.

Interest depends on comprehension.--First of all we must remember that ***interest never attaches to what the mind does not grasp***. Go yourself and listen to the technical lecture you do not understand, or try to read the book that deals with matters concerning which you have no information; then apply the results of your experience to the case of the child. The matter we teach the child must have sufficient connection with his own experience, be sufficiently close to the things he knows and cares about, so that he has a basis on which to comprehend them. The ***new*** must be related to something ***old and familiar*** in the mind to meet a warm welcome.

If we would secure the child's interest, we must make certain of a "point of contact" in his own life and meet him on the plane of his own experience. God smiling in the sunshine, making the flowers grow or whispering in the breeze is closer to the child than God as "Creator." God protecting and watching over the child timid and afraid in the dark is more real than God in his heaven as "protec-tor." We must remember that not what *we* feel is of value, but ***what the child feels is of value*** is what will appeal to his interest and attention. And no exertion or agonizing on our part will create interest in the child in matters for which his own understanding and experience have not fitted him. For example, probably no child is ever interested in learning the church catechism or Bible verses which we prize so highly, but which he can not understand nor apply; he may be interested in a prize to be had at the end of the learning, but in this case the interest is in the reward and not in the matter learned. ***Empty words devoid of meaning never fire interest nor kindle enthusiasm.***

Interest attaches to action.--Children are interested more in action, deeds, and events than in motives, reasons, and explanations. They care more for the uses to which objects are to be put than for the objects themselves.

No boy is interested in a bicycle chiefly as an example of mechanical skill, but, rather, as a means of locomotion. No girl is interested in dolls just as dolls, nor as a product of the toy maker's skill, but to play with. It is this quality that makes chil-dren respond to the story, for the story deals with action instead of with explana-tion and description. In the story there is life and movement, and not reasoning and mere assertion. The story presents the lesson in terms of deeds and events, instead of by means of abstract statement and formal conclusion.

This principle carries over to the child's own participation. Everyone is most interested in that in which he has an active part. The meeting in which we presided or made a speech or presented a report is to us a more interesting meeting than one in which we were a silent auditor. To the child, personal response is even more necessary. No small part of the reason why the child "learns by doing" is that he is interested in doing as he is not interested in mere listening. All good teaching will therefore appeal to interest through providing the fullest possible opportunity for the child to have an important share in the lesson. And this part must be something which *to the child* is worth doing, and not, for example, an oral memory drill on words meaningless to the pupil, nor "expression" work of a kind that lacks purpose and action. There are always real things to be done if the lesson is vital--personal experiences to be recounted, special assignments to be reported upon, maps to be drawn or remodeled, specimens of flowers or plants to be secured, character parts to be represented in the story, a bit of history to be looked up, prayers to be said, songs to be sung, or a hundred other things done which will appeal to the interest and at the same time fix the points of the lesson.

Interest requires variety and change.--Interest attaches to the *new*, provided the new is sufficiently related to the fund of experience already on hand so that it is fully grasped and understood. While there are certain matters, such as marching, handling supplies, etc., in the recitation which should be done the same way each time so that they may become habit and routine, yet there is a wide range of variety possible in much of the procedure.

The lessons should not be conducted always in the same way. One recitation may consist chiefly of discussion, with question and answer between teacher and class. Another may be given largely to reports on special assignments, with the teacher's comments to broaden and apply the points. Another may take the form of stories told and illustrations given by the teacher, or of stories retold by the class from former lessons. The great thing is to secure change and variety without losing sight of the real aims of the lesson, and to plan for a pleasant surprise now and then without lowering the value of the instruction.

Interest is contagious.--Every observing teacher has learned that interest is contagious. An interested and enthusiastic teacher is seldom troubled by lack of interest and attention on the part of the class. Nor, on the other hand, will interest and attention continue on the part of the class if confronted by a mechanical and lifeless teacher. The teacher is the model unconsciously accepted and responded to by his class. He leads the way in interest and enthusiasm. Nor will any sham or pretense serve. The interest must be real and deep. Even young children quickly sense any make-believe enthusiasm or vivacity on the part of the teacher, and their ardor immediately cools.

Children's typical interests have their birth, ripen to full strength, and fade away by certain broad stages. What will appeal to the child of five will not appeal to the child of ten, and will secure no response from the youth of fifteen. Space will not permit even an outline of these interest-stages here, but genetic psychology has carefully mapped them out and their nature and order of development should be studied by every teacher.

FREEDOM FROM DISTRACTIONS

There is no possibility of securing good results from a lesson period constantly broken in upon by distractions. The mind cannot do its best work if the attention is diverted every few moments from the train of thought, requiring a new start every now and then. Every teacher has had the experience of the sudden drop in interest and concentration that has come from some interruption, and the impossibility of bringing the class back to the former level after the break. The loss in a recitation disturbed by distractions is comparable to the loss of power and efficiency in stopping a train of cars every half mile throughout its run instead of allowing it an unbroken trip. Careful planning and good management can eliminate many of the distractions common to the church school lesson hour.

Distractions from classes reciting together.--The class should have a room or space for its own sole use, and not be compelled to recite in a large room occupied by several other classes. The older Chinese method of education was to have each pupil study his lesson aloud, each seeking to drown out the confusion by the force of his voice. Many of our church schools of the present day remind one of this ancient method. The church building being planned primarily for adults, not enough classrooms are provided for the children, and it is a common thing to find half a dozen classes grouped in the one room, each constantly distracted by the sights and sounds that so insistently appeal to the senses. It is wholly impossible to do really good teaching under such conditions.

Every church building should provide classrooms for teaching its children. If these cannot be had in the original edifice, an addition should be made of a special school building. As a last resort, a system of curtains or movable partitions should be provided which will isolate each class from every other class, and thereby save at least the visual distractions and perhaps a part of the auditory distractions. To fail to do this is to cultivate in the child a habit of inattention to the lesson, and to kill his interest in the church school and its work because of its failure to impress him or attract his loyalty.

Planning routine to prevent distractions.--Not infrequently a wholly unnecessary distraction is caused by a poorly planned method of handling certain routine matters. The writer recently observed a junior class get under way in what promised to be a very interesting and profitable lesson. They had an attractive lesson theme, a good teacher, a separate classroom, and seemed to be mentally alert. Soon after the lesson had got well started an officer appeared at the door with an envelope for the collection, and the story was stopped to pass the envelope around the class. It was not possible after this interruption to pick up the thread of the lesson without some loss of interest, but the teacher was skillful and did her best. She soon had the attention of the class again and the lesson was moving along toward its most interesting part and the practical application. But just at the most critical moment another interruption occurred; the secretary came in with the papers for the class and counted out the necessary supply while the class looked on. It was impossible now to catch up the current of interest again, but the teacher tried. Once more she was interrupted, however, this time by a note containing some announcement that had been overlooked in the opening exercises!

All such interruptions as these indicate mismanagement and a serious lack of foresight. The fault is not wholly with the teacher, but also with the policy and organization of the school as a whole. The remedy is for both officers and teachers to use the same business sense and ability in running the church school that they would apply to any other concern. The collection can be taken at the beginning of the lesson period. The papers and lesson material can be in the classroom or in the teacher's hands before the class assembles, and not require distribution during the lesson period. In short, all matters of routine can be so carefully foreseen and provided for that the class will be wholly free from all unnecessary distractions from such sources.

Mischief and disorder.--An especially difficult kind of distraction to control is the tendency to restlessness, mischief, and misbehavior which prevails in certain classes or on the part of an occasional pupil. Pupils sometimes feel that the teacher in the church school does not possess the same authority as that exercised by the public-school teacher, and so take advantage of this fact. The first safeguard against disorder in the class is, of course, to secure the interest and loyalty of the members. The ideal is for the children to be attentive, respectful, and well behaved, not because they are required to, but because their sense of duty and pride and their interest in the work leads them to this kind of conduct. It is not possible, however, continuously to reach this ideal with all children. There will be occasional cases of tendency to disorder, and the spirit of mischief will sometimes take possession of a class whose conduct is otherwise good.

Whenever it becomes necessary, the teacher should not hesitate to take a positive stand for order and quiet in the class. All inattention is contagious. A small center of disturbance can easily spread until it results in a whole storm of disorder. Mischief grows through the power of suggestion, and a small beginning may soon involve a whole class. There is no place for a spirit of irreverence and boisterousness in the church school, and the teacher must have for one of his first principles the maintenance of good conduct in his classroom. No one can tell any teacher just how this is to be achieved in individual cases, but it must be done. And the teacher who cannot win control over his class would better surrender it to another who has more of the quality of leadership or mastery in his make-up, for no worthy, lasting religious impressions can be given to noisy, boisterous, and inattentive children.

Distractions by the teacher.--Strange as it may seem, the teacher may himself be a distraction in the classroom. Any striking mannerism, any peculiarity of manner or carriage, extreme types of dress, or any personal quality that attracts attention to itself is a distraction to the class. One teacher may have a very loud or ill-modulated voice; another may speak too low to be heard without too much effort; another may fail to articulate clearly. Whatever attracts attention to the speech itself draws attention away from the thought back of the speech and hinders the listener from giving his full powers to the lesson.

A distracting habit on the part of some teachers is to walk back and forth before the class, or to assume awkward postures in standing or sitting before the class, or nervously to finger a book or some object held in the hands. All these may seem like small things, but success or failure often depends upon a conjunction of many small things, each of which in itself may seem unimportant. It is often "the little foxes that spoil the vines."

Avoiding physical distractions.--In the church school, as in the public school, the physical conditions surrounding the recitation should be made as favorable as possible. Not infrequently the children are placed for their lesson hour in seats that were intended for adults, and which are extremely uncomfortable for smaller persons. The children's feet do not touch the floor, and their backs can not secure a support; weariness, wriggling and unrest are sure to follow. Sometimes the ventilation of the classroom is bad, and the foul air breathed on one Sunday is carefully shut in for use the next. Basement rooms are not seldom damp, or they have a bad odor, or the lighting is unsatisfactory, or the walls are streaked, dim and uninviting. If such things seem relatively unimportant, we must remember that the child's spiritual life is closely tied up with the whole range of his experiences, and that such things as lack of oxygen in the classroom, tired legs whose feet can not touch the floor, eyes offended by unloveliness, or nostrils assailed by unpleasant odors may get in the way of the soul's development. Our churches should not rest satisfied until children in the church schools work under as hygienic and as pleasant conditions as obtain in the best of our public schools.

DANGER POINTS IN INSTRUCTION

It is a well-known law in pedagogy that negatives are not often inspiring, and that to hold before one his mistakes is not always the best way of helping him avoid them. Along with the positive principles which show what we should do, however, it is well occasionally to note a few of the danger points most commonly met in the classroom.

Lack of definiteness.--This may take the form of lack of definiteness of aim or purpose. We may merely "hear" the recitation, or ask the stock questions furnished in the lesson helps, or allow the discussion to wander where it will, or permit aimless arguing or disputing on questions that cannot be decided and that in any case possess no real significance.

Indefiniteness may take the direction of failure to carry the thoughts of the lesson through to their final meaning and application, so that there is no vital connection made between the lesson truths and the lives of those we teach. Or we may be indefinite in our interpretation of the moral and religious values inherent in the lesson, and so fail to make a sharp and definite impression of understanding and conviction on our pupils. Our teaching must be clear-cut and positive without being narrowly dogmatic or opinionated. The truth we present must have an edge, so that it may cleave its way into the heart and mind of the learner.

Dead levels.--We need to avoid ***dead levels*** in our teaching. This danger arises from lack of mental perspective. It comes from presenting all the points of a lesson on the same ***plane of emphasis***, with a failure to distinguish between the important and the unimportant. Minor details and incidental aspects of the topic often receive the same degree of stress that is given to more important points. This results in a state of monotonous plodding through so much material without responding to its varying shades of meaning and value. Not only does this type of teaching fail to lodge in the mind of the pupil the larger and more important truths which ought to become a permanent part of his mental equipment, but it also fails to train pupils how themselves to pick out and appropriate the significant parts of the lesson material. It does not develop the sense of value for lesson truths which should be trained through the work of the lesson hour. Each lesson should seek to impress and apply a few important truths, and everything else should be made to work to this end. The points we would have our pupils remember, think about and act upon we must be able to make stand out above all other aspects of the lesson; they must not, for want of emphasis, be lost in a mass of irrelevant or monotonous material of little value.

Lack of movement in recitation.--Some recitations suffer from ***slowness of movement*** of the thought and plan of the lesson. We sometimes say of a book or a play or a sermon that it was "slow." This is equivalent to saying that the book or play or sermon lacks movement; it dallies by the way, and has unnecessary breaks in its continuity, or is slow in its action. The same principle applies in the recitation. Pauses that are occupied with thought or meditation are not, of course, wasted; they may even be the very best part of the lesson period. But the rather empty lapses which occur for no reason except that the teacher lacks readiness and preparation, and does not quite know at every moment just what he is to do next, or what topic should at this moment come in--it is such awkward and meaningless breaks as these that spoil the continuity of thought and interest and result in boredom. We must remember that every pause or interval of mere empty waiting without expectancy, or without some worthy thought occupying the mind, is a waste of energy, time, and opportunity, and also a training in inattention.

Low standards.--The acceptance of ***low standards*** of preparation and response in the recitation is fatal to high-grade work and results. If it comes to be expected and taken as a matter of course both by teacher and pupils that children shall come to the class from week to week with no previous study on the lesson, then this is precisely what they will do. The standards of the class should make it impossible that continual failure to prepare or recite shall be accepted as the natural and expected thing, or treated with a spirit of levity. The lesson hour is the very heart and center of the school work, and failure here means a breakdown of the whole system. The standards of teacher and class should be such that probable failure to do one's part in the recitation shall be looked forward to by the child with some apprehension and looked back upon with some regret if not humiliation. In order to maintain high standards of preparation the cooperation of the home must be secured, at least for the younger children, and parents must help the child wisely and sympathetically in the study of the lesson.

1. To what extent are you able to hold the attention of your pupils in the recitation? Is their attention ready, or do you have to work hard to get it? Are there any particular ones who are less attentive than the rest? If so, can you discover the reason? The remedy?

2. To what extent do you find it necessary to appeal to involuntary attention? If you have to make such an appeal do you seek at once to make interest take hold to retain the attention?

3. What measures are you using to train your pupils in the giving of voluntary attention when this type is required? When *is* voluntary attention required?

4. How completely are your pupils usually interested in the lessons? As the interest varies from time to time, are you studying the matter to discover the secret of interest on their part. In so far as interest fails, which of the factors discussed in the section on interest in this chapter are related to the failure? Are there still other causes not mentioned in this chapter?

5. What distractions are most common in your class? Can you discover the cause? The remedy? Do you have any unruly pupils? If so, have you done your best to win to attention and interest? Have you the force and decision necessary to bring the class well under control?

6. What do you consider your chief danger points in teaching? Would it be worth while for you to have some sympathetic teacher friend visit your class while you teach, and then later talk over with you the points in which you could improve?

FOR FURTHER READING
Bagley, Class Room Management.
Betts, The Recitation.
Maxwell, The Observation of Teaching.
Strayer and Norsworthy, How to Teach.
Weigle, The Pupil and the Teacher.

CHAPTER X
MAKING TRUTH VIVID

L ife is a great unbreakable unity. Thought, feeling, and action belong together, and to leave out one destroys the quality and significance of all. Religious growth and development involve the same mental powers that are used in the other affairs of life. The child's training in religion can advance no faster than the expansion of his grasp of thought and comprehension, the deepening of his emotions, and the strengthening of his will.

It follows from this that religious instruction must call for and use the same activities of mind that are called for in other phases of education. Not only must the feelings be reached and the emotions stirred, but the child must be taught to *think* in his religion. Not only must trust and faith be grounded, but these must be made *intelligent*. Not only must the spirit of worship be cultivated, but the child must know Whom and why he worships. Not only must loyalties be secured, but these must grow out of a *realization of the cost and worth* of the cause or object to which loyalty attaches. Religious teaching must therefore appeal to the *whole* mind. Besides appealing to the emotions and will it must make use of and train the power of *thought*, of *imagination*, of *memory*; it must through their agency make truth vivid, real, and lasting, and so lay the foundation for spiritual feeling and devotion.

LEARNING TO THINK IN RELIGION

Much has been gained in teaching religion when we have brought the child to see that ***understanding***, ***reason***, and ***common sense*** are as necessary and as possible here as in other fields of learning. This does not mean that there are not many things in religion that are beyond the grasp and comprehension of even the greatest minds, to say nothing of the undeveloped mind of the child. It means, rather, that where we fail to grasp or understand it is because of the bigness of the problem, or because of its unknowableness, and not because its solution violates the laws of thought and reason.

The reign of law, the inexorable working of cause and effect, and the application of reason to religious matters should be conveyed to the child in his earliest impressions of religion. For example, the child has learned a valuable lesson when he has comprehended that God asks obedience of his children, not just for the sake of compelling obedience, but because obedience to God's law is the only way to happy and successful living. The youth has grasped a great truth when it becomes clear to his understanding that Jesus said, "To him that hath shall be given," not from any failure to sympathize with the one who might be short in his share, but ***because this is the great and fundamental law of being*** to which even Jesus himself was subject; and that when Paul said, "Whatsoever a man soweth, that shall he also reap," he was not exacting an arbitrary penalty, but expressing the inevitable working of a great law. The boy who defined faith as "believing something you know can't be true" had been badly taught concerning faith.

Religious truth does not contradict reason.--To begin with, while all of us come to believe many things that we cannot fully understand, not even the child should be asked to believe what plainly contradicts common sense and so puts too great a strain on credulity. In a certain Sunday school class the lesson was about Peter going up on the housetop to pray, and the vision that befell him there. This class of boys, living in a small village, had had no experience with any kind of housetop except that formed of a sharply sloping roof. Therefore the story looked improbable to them, and one boy asked how Peter could sleep up on the roof and keep from falling off. The teacher, also uninformed concerning the flat roofs of Oriental houses, answered, "John, you must remember that with God all things are possible." And John had that day had the seeds of skepticism planted in his inquiring mind. Another teacher, thinking to allay any tendency on the part of his class to question the literal accuracy of the story of Jonah and the whale, said, "This story is in the Bible, and we must believe it, for whatever is in the Bible is true; and if the Bible were to say that Jonah swallowed the whale that would be true, and we would have to believe that also." But who can doubt that, with boys and girls trained in the schools and by their contact with life itself to think, such an invitation to lay aside all reason and common sense can do other in the long run than to weaken confidence in the Bible, and so lessen the significance of many of its beautiful lessons?

True thinking about Bible truths.--What, then, shall we teach the child about the literalness of the Bible? Nothing. This is not a question for childhood. The Bible should be brought to the child in the same spirit as any other book, except with a deep spirit of reverence and appreciation not due other books. Parts of the Bible are plainly history, and as accurate as history of other kinds is. Other parts are accounts of the lives of people, and the descriptions are wonderfully vivid and true to life. Other parts are plainly poetry, and should be read and interpreted as poetry. Other parts are clearly the stories and legends current in the days when the accounts were written, and should be read as other stories and legends are read. The great question is not the problem of the literal or the figurative nature of the truth, but the problem of discovering for the child the *rich nugget of spiritual wisdom which is always there*.

When the young child first hears the entrancing Bible stories he does not think anything about their literalness; he only enjoys, and perhaps dimly senses the hidden lesson or truth they contain. This is as it should be. Later, when thought, judgment, and discrimination are developing and beginning to play their part in the expanding mind, questions are sure to arise at certain points. This is also as it should be.

When such questions arise let us meet them frankly and wisely. Let us have the spiritual vision and the reverence for truth that will enable us, for example, to show the child how the servants of God in those ancient times used the bold, picturesque figure of "feathers" and "wings" to express the brooding love and care of God; how they told the wonderful story of God's creation of the world in the most beautiful account they could conceive; how they showed forth God's care for his children, his companionship with them, and man's tendency to sin and disobedience by one of the most beautiful stories ever written, this story having its scene laid in the garden of Eden; how these writers always set down what they believed to be true, and how, though they might sometimes have been mistaken as to the actual facts, they never missed presenting the great lesson or deep spiritual truth that God would have us know.

Protecting the child against intellectual difficulties.--Children taught the Bible in this reasonable but reverent way will be saved many intellectual difficulties as they grow older. Their reverence and respect for the Bible will never suffer from the necessity of attempting to force their faith to accept what their intellect contradicts. They will not be troubled by the grave doubts and misgivings which attack so many adolescents during the time when they are working out their mental and spiritual adjustment to the new world of individual responsibility which they have discovered. They will, without strain or questioning, come to accept the Bible for what it is--the great *Source Book of spiritual wisdom*, its pages bearing the imprint of divine inspiration and guidance, and also of human imperfections and greatness.

The developing child should, therefore, be encouraged to use his reason, his thought, his judgment and discrimination in his study of religion precisely as in other things. His questions should never be ignored, nor suppressed, nor treated as something unworthy and sinful. The doubts, even, which are somewhat characteristic of a stage of adolescent reconstruction, may be made the stepping-stone to higher reaches of faith and understanding.

The youth who went to his pastor with certain questionings and doubts, and who was told that these were "the promptings of Satan," and that they "must not be dwelt upon, but resolutely be put out of the mind," was not fairly nor honestly treated by one from whom he had a right to expect wiser guidance. He returned from the interview rebellious and bitter, and it was with much spiritual agony and sweating of blood that he fought his own way through to a solution which ought to have been made easy for him by wise enlightenment and sympathetic counsel.

Reverent seekers after truth.--Religion requires the mind at its best. There is nothing about religion that will not bear full thought and investigation. We are not asked to lay aside any part of our powers, can not lay any part of them aside, if we would attain to full religious growth and stature. Let us therefore train our children to *think* as they study religion. Let us lead them to ask and inquire. Let us train them to investigate and test. Let us teach them that they never need be afraid of truth, since no bit of truth ever conflicts with, or contradicts any other truth; let us rather encourage them reverently and with open hearts and minds diligently to seek the truth, and then *dare to follow where it leads*.

THE APPEAL TO IMAGINATION

Imagination, the power of the mind that pictures and makes real, is a key to vivid and lasting impressions. Unless the imagination recreates the scenes described in the story, or vivifies the events of the lesson, they will have little meaning to the child and appeal but little to his interest.

It is imagination that enables its possessor to take the images suggested in the account of a battle and build them together into the mass of struggling soldiers, roaring cannon, whistling bullets, and bursting shells. It is imagination that makes it possible while reading the words of the poem to construct the picture which was in the mind of the author as he wrote "The Village Blacksmith," the twenty-third psalm, or "Snowbound," and thereby enables the reader himself to take part in the throbbing scenes of life and action. Without imagination one may repeat the words which describe an act or an event, may even commit them to memory or pass an examination upon them, but the living reality will forever escape him. It is imagination that will save the beautiful stories and narratives of the Bible from being so many dead words, without appeal to the child.

Imagination required in the study of religion.--In the teaching of religion we are especially dependent on the child's use of his imagination. With younger children the instruction largely takes the form of stories, which must be appropriated and understood through the imagination or not at all. The whole Bible account deals with people, places, and events distant in time and strange to the child in manner of life and customs. The Bible itself abounds in pictorial descriptions. The missionary enterprises of the church lead into strange lands and introduce strange people. The study of the lives and characters of great men and women and their deeds of service in our own land takes the child out of the range of his own immediate observation and experience. The understanding of God and of Jesus--all of these things lose in significance or are in large degree incomprehensible unless approached with a vivid and glowing imagination.

Many older persons confess that the Bible times, places, and people were all very unreal to them while in the Sunday school, and that it hardly occurred to them that these descriptions and narratives were truly about men and women like ourselves. Hence the most valuable part of their instruction was lost.

Limitations of imagination.--Since childhood is the age of imagination, we might naturally expect that it would be no trouble to secure ready response from the child's imagination. But we must not assume too much about the early power of imagination. It is true that the child's imagination is *ready and active*; but it is not yet ready for the more difficult and complex picturing we sometimes require of it, for imagination depends for its material on the store of *images* accumulated from former experience; and images are the result of past observation, of percepts, and sensory experiences. The imagination can build no mental structures without the stuff with which to build; it is limited to the material on hand. The Indians never dreamed of a heaven with streets of gold and a great white throne; for their experiences had given them no knowledge of such things. They therefore made their heaven out of the "Happy Hunting Grounds," of which they had many images.

Many Chicago school children who were asked to compare the height of a mountain with that of a tall factory chimney said that the chimney was higher, because the mountain "does not go straight up" like the chimney. These children had learned and recited that a mountain "is an elevation of land a thousand or more than a thousand feet in height," but their imagination failed to picture the mountain, since not even the smallest mountain nor a high hill had ever been actually present to their observation. Small wonder, then, that Sunday school children have some trouble, living as they do in these modern times, to picture ancient times and peoples who were so different from any with which their experience has had to deal!

Guiding principles.--The skillful teacher knows how to help the child use his imagination. The following laws or principles will aid in such training:

1. ***Relate the new scene or picture with something similar in the child's experience.*** The desert is like the sandy waste or the barren and stony hillside with which the children are acquainted. The square, flat-topped houses of eastern lands have their approximate counterpart in occasional buildings to be found in almost any modern community. The rivers and lakes of Bible lands may be compared with rivers and lakes near at hand. The manner of cooking and serving food under primitive conditions was not so different from our own method on picnics and excursion days. While the life and work of the shepherd have changed, we still have the sheep. The walls of the ancient city can be seen in miniature in stone and concrete embankments, or even the stone fences common in some sections.

The main thing is to get some ***starting point*** in actual observation from which the child can proceed. The teacher must then help the child to modify from the actual in such a way as to picture the object or place described as nearly true to reality as possible. The child who said, "A mountain is a mound of earth with brush growing on it" had been shown a hillock covered with growing brush and had been told that the mountain was like this, only bigger. The imagination had not been sufficiently stimulated to realize the significant differences and to picture the real mountain from the miniature suggestion.

2. ***Articles and objects from ancient times or from other lands may occasionally be secured to show the children.*** Even if such objects may not date back to Bible times, they are still useful as a vantage point for the imagination. A modern copy of the old-time Oriental lamp, a candelabrum, a pair of sandals, a turban, a robe, or garment such as the ancients wore--these accompanied by intelligent description of the times and places to which they belonged are all a stimulus to the child's imagination which should not be overlooked. The very fact that they suggest other peoples and other modes of living than our own is an invitation and incentive to the mind to reach out beyond the immediate and the familiar to the new and the strange.

3. ***Pictures can be made a great help to the imagination.*** In the better type of our church schools we are now making free use of pictures as teaching material. It is not always enough, however, merely to place the picture before the child. It requires a certain fund of information and interest in order to see in a picture what

it is intended to convey. The child cannot get from the picture more than he brings to it. The teacher may therefore need to give the picture its proper setting by describing the kind of life or the type of action or event with which it deals. He may need to ask questions, and make suggestions in order to be sure that the child sees in the picture the interesting and important things, and that his imagination carries out beyond what is actually presented in the picture itself to what it suggests. While the first response of the child to a picture, as to a story, should be that of enjoyment and interest, this does not mean that the picture, like the story, may not reach much deeper than the immediate interest and enjoyment. The picture which has failed to stimulate the child's imagination to see much more than the picture contains has failed of one of its chief objects.

4. *Stimulate the imagination by use of vivid descriptions and thought-provoking questions.* Every teacher, whether of young children or of older ones, should strive to be a good teller of stories and a good user of illustrations. This requires study and practice, but it is worth the cost--even outside of the classroom. The good story-teller must be able to speak freely, easily, and naturally. He must have a sense of the important and significant in a story or illustration, and be able to work to a climax. He must know just how much of detail to use to appeal to the imagination to supply the remainder, and not employ so great an amount of detail as to leave nothing to the imagination of the listener. He must himself enter fully into the spirit and enthusiasm of the story, and must have his own imagination filled with the pictures he would create in his pupils' minds. He must himself enjoy the story or the illustration, and thus be able in his expression and manner to suggest the response he desires from the children. Well told stories that have in them the dramatic quality can hardly fail to stir the most sluggish imagination and prepare it for the important part it must play in the child's religious development.

Skillfully used questions and suggestions can be made an important means of stimulating the imagination. Such helps as: Do you think the sea of Galilee looked like the lake (here name one near at hand) which you know? How did it differ? What tree have you in mind which is about the same size as the fig tree in the lesson? How does it differ in appearance? Close your eyes and try to see in your mind just how the river looked where the baby Moses was found. Have you ever seen a man who you think looks much as Elijah must have looked? Describe him. If you were going to make a coat like the one Joseph wore, what colors would you select? What kind of cloth? What would be the cut or shape of it?--Hardly a lesson period will pass without many opportunities for wise questions whose chief purpose is to make real and vivid to the child the persons or places described, and so add to their significance to him.

5. *Dramatic representation can be used as an incentive to the imagination.* Children easily and naturally imagine themselves to be some other person, and often play at being nurse or school teacher or doctor or preacher. Nearly every child possesses a large measure of the dramatic impulse, and is something of an actor. It is great fun for children to "tog up" and to "show off" in their play. And not only is all this an expression of imagination actively at work, but such activities are themselves a great stimulus to the imagination. The child who has dressed up as George Washington and impersonated him in some ceremonial or on a public occasion will ever after feel a closer reality in the life and work of Washington than would come from mere reading about him. A group of children who have acted out the story of the good Samaritan will get a little closer to its inner meaning than merely to hear the story told. The girl who has taken the part of Esther appearing before the king in behalf of her people will realize a little more fully from that experience what devotion and courage were required from the real Esther. A class who have participated in a pageant of the Nativity will always be a little nearer to the original event than if their imaginations had not been called upon to make real the characters and incidents.

USING THE MEMORY

The memory should play an important part in religion. Gems from the Bible, stories, characters, and events, inspiring thoughts and maxims, and many other such things should become a permanent part of the furnishing of the mind, recorded and faithfully preserved by the memory.

Laws of use of memory.--The laws by which the memory works have been thoroughly studied and carefully described, and should be fully understood by every teacher. Further than this, *they should be faithfully observed in all memory work*. These laws may be stated as follows:

1. The law of *complete registration*. The first act in the memory process is fully and completely to register, or *learn*, the matter to be retained. The retention can never be better than the registration of the facts given into the memory's keeping. Half-learned matter easily slips away, never having been completely impressed on the mind. It is possible to lose both effort and efficiency by committing a verse of a poem barely up to the point where it can doubtfully be repeated instead of giving it the relatively small amount of additional study and practice which would register it firmly and completely. Whatever is worth committing to memory should therefore be carried past the barely known stage and committed fully and completely.

2. The law of *multiple association*. This only means that the new facts learned shall be related as closely as may be to matter already in the mind. And this is equivalent to saying that the material learned shall be *understood*, its meaning grasped and its significance comprehended. To understand for yourself the value of association, make this experiment: Have some one write down a list of ten unrelated words in a column, and hold the list before you while you have time to read it over just once slowly and carefully. Now try repeating the words in order from memory. Next, have your friend write ten other words which this time form a connected sentence. After reading these words over once as you did the first list, try repeating them in order. You find that you have much trouble to memorize the first list, while the second presents no difficulty at all. The difference lies in the fact that the words of the first list were unrelated, lacking all associative connections with each other, while those of the second list formed a connected chain of associations.

It is possible to give the child biblical or other matter to memorize that has little more meaning to him than the list of unrelated words have to us. For example, this text is required of primary and junior children in a lesson series: "Ye shall know the truth, and the truth shall make you free." And this: "Let us therefore draw near with boldness unto the throne of grace, that we may receive mercy, and may find grace to help us in time of need." It is evident that younger children could by no possibility understand either of these beautiful passages, and hence in committing them will only be learning so many unrelated words.

The same is true of church catechisms. The memorizing of such material will be difficult and unpleasant, and no value will come from it. The most likely outcome of such ill-advised requirements is to discourage the child and make him dislike the church school and all its work. It is not to be expected that the child will understand the *full* meaning of every bit of matter suitable for him to memorize; this will have to await broader experience and fuller development. The material should, however, be sufficiently comprehended that its general meaning is clear and its significance understood.

3. The law of *vividness of impression*. The relation of vividness of impression to learning has already been discussed in another chapter. In no one of the mind's activities is vividness a more important factor than in memorizing. Matter committed under the stimulus of high interest and keen attention is relatively secure, while matter committed under slack concentration is sure to fade quickly from the memory. Songs can therefore best be committed under the elation of the interesting singing of the words; a verse of poetry, when the mind is alert and the feelings aroused by a story in which the sentiment of the verse fits; a prayer when the spirit of devotion has been quickened by worship. To insure full vividness the imagination must also be called upon to picture and make real such parts of memory material as contain imagery.

4. The law of *repetition*. For most minds memory depends on repetition. The impressions must be deepened and made lasting by being stamped again and again on the mind. The neurons of the brain which do the work of retaining and recalling must be made to repeat the process over and over until their action is secure. It is therefore not enough to make sure that the child has his memory material committed for this particular Sunday. If the matter was worth committing in the first place, it is worth keeping permanently. If it is to be kept permanently, it must be frequently reviewed; for otherwise it will surely be forgotten. It is to be feared that much, if not most, of the matter memorized by the pupils in many church schools lasts only long enough to show the teacher that it has once been learned, and that not many children know in any permanent sense the Bible passages they have committed. In so far as this is true it would be much better to select a smaller amount of the choicest and best adapted material to be found, and then so thoroughly teach this that it is permanently retained.

5. The law of *wholes instead of parts*. Many persons in setting at work to commit a poem, a Bible passage, a psalm have a tendency to learn it first by verses or

sections and then, put the parts together to form the whole. Tests upon the memory have shown, that this is a less economical and efficient method than from the first to commit the material as a whole. This method requires that we go over all of it completely from beginning to end, then over it again, and so on until we can repeat much of it without reference to the text. We then refer to the text for what the memory has not yet grasped, requiring the memory to repeat all that has been committed, until the whole is in this manner fully learned. The method of learning by wholes not only requires less time and effort, but gives a better sense of unity in the matter committed.

6. The law of ***divided practice***. If to learn a certain piece of material the child must go over it, say, fifteen times, the results are much better if the whole number of repetitions are not carried out at one time. Time seems necessary to give the associations an opportunity to set up their relationships; also, the interval between repetitions allows the parts that are hardest to commit to begin fading out, and thereby reveal where further practice is demanded. Where songs, Bible verses, or other material are committed in the lesson hour, provision ought to be made for the children to continue study and practice on the material at home during the week. The so-called cramming process of learning will not work any better in the church school than in the day-school lessons.

7. The law of ***motivation***. Like other activities of the mind, memory works best under the stimulus of some appealing motive. The very best possible motive is, of course, an interest in and love for the matter committed. This kind of response can hardly be expected, however, in all of the material children are asked to commit. It is necessary to use additional motives to secure full effort. The approval of the teacher and parents, the child's standing in the class, and his own sense of achievement are some of the motives that should be employed.

A very powerful motive not always sufficiently made use of is the wider ***social motive*** that comes from working in groups for a particular end. For example, a school or class pageant based on some biblical story or religious event has the effect of centralizing effort and stimulating endeavor to a degree impossible in individual work. Hymns and songs are committed, Bible passages or other religious material learned, stories mastered, characters studied and their words committed under the stress of an immediate need for them in order to take one's part in a social group and prove one's mastery before an audience of interested listeners. The church school can with great advantage centralize more of its religious memory work in preparation for such special occasions as Easter, Christmas, Thanksgiving, or other church celebrations or pageants.

1. What reasons can you give why children should be taught to think in their study of religion just as in the study of any other subject? Do you find a thoughtful attitude on the part of your class? What methods do you use to encourage reverent thinking in religion?

2. One thinks best in connection with some question or problem which he wishes to have answered. Do you plan in connection with your preparation of the lesson to bring out some definite problem suited to the age of your class and help your pupils think it through to a solution?

3. What evidences can you suggest from your class work which show that children readily think upon any problem that interests them? Have your pupils asked questions showing that they are thinking? When such questions are asked, how do you treat them?

4. What lessons of recent date in your work have you in mind which especially required the use of imagination? Can you judge the degree to which the descriptive parts of the lessons appeal to your pupils as real?

5. How successfully do you feel that you are applying the principles for the use of the imagination? Do you definitely seek to apply these principles in your lessons? Which of these is probably the hardest to apply? What is your method of seeking its application?

6. Are your pupils good in memory work? Do you ever give them material to memorize the meaning of which is not wholly clear to them? What help do you give the children when you assign them memory work? Do you instruct them how to memorize what you assign? To what extent are you following the laws of memory as stated in the chapter?

FOR FURTHER READING
Betts, The Mind and Its Education.
Dewey, How We Think.
Coe, Education in Religion and Morals.

CHAPTER XI
TYPES OF TEACHING

One of the surest tests of the skillful teacher is his ability to adapt his instruction to the child, to the subject matter, and to the occasion--that is, to the *aim*. Teaching must differ in its type with the age; the primary child and the older youth require different methods. It must differ with the kind of material to be presented; a lesson whose chief aim is to give information must be differently presented from a lesson whose aim is to enforce some moral or religious truth. It must differ with the occasion; a lesson taught a group of children who have had no previous study or preparation on it will demand different treatment from a lesson which has had careful study.

Types of lessons.--Several clearly recognized types of lessons are commonly employed by teachers in both school and church-school classes. No one of these lesson types can be said to be best in the sense that it should be used to the exclusion of the others. All are required. Several may even be employed in the same recitation period. The teacher should, however, know which type he is employing at any given stage of his instruction, and why he is using this type in preference to another type of teaching. The following are the chief lesson types that will be found serviceable in most church school classes:

1. The *informational* lesson; in which the immediate aim is to supply the mind with new knowledge or facts needed as a part of the equipment of thought and understanding.

2. The *developmental* (or inductive) lesson; in which the aim is to lead the child through his own investigation and thinking to use the information already in his possession as a basis for discovering new truth or meaning.

3. The ***application*** (or deductive) lesson; in which the aim is to make application of some general truth or lesson already known to particular problems or cases.

4. The ***drill*** lesson; in which the aim is to give readiness and skill in fundamental facts or material that should be so well known as to be practically automatic in thought or memory.

5. The ***appreciation*** lesson; in which the aim is to create a response of warmth and interest toward, or appreciation of, a person, object, situation, or the material studied.

6. The ***review*** lesson; in, which the aim is to gather up, relate, and fix more permanently in the mind the lessons or facts that have been studied.

7. The ***assignment*** lesson; in which help is rendered and interest inspired, for study of the next lesson.

THE INFORMATIONAL LESSON

The child at the beginning is devoid of all knowledge of and information about the many objects, activities, and relationships that fill his world. He must come to know these. His mind can develop no faster than it has the materials for thoughts, memories, ideas, and whatever else is to occupy his stream of thought. He must therefore be supplied with information. He must be given a fund of impressions, of facts, of knowledge to use in his thinking, feeling, and understanding.

To undertake to teach the child the deeper meanings and relationships of God to our lives without this necessary background of information is to confuse him and to fail ourselves as teachers. For example, a certain primary lesson leaflet tells the children that the Egyptians made slaves out of the Israelites and that God led the Israelites out of this slavery. But there had previously been no adequate preparation of the learners' minds to understand who the Israelites or the Egyptians were, nor what slavery is. The children lacked all basis of information to understand the situation described, and it could by no possibility possess meaning for them.

The use of the information lesson.--It is not meant, of course, that when the chief purpose of a lesson is to give information no applications should be made or no interpretations given of the matter presented. Yet the fact is that often the chief emphasis must be placed on information, and that for the moment other aims are secondary. To illustrate: When young children are first told the story of God creating the world the main purpose of the lesson is ***just to give them the story***, and not to attempt instruction as to the power and wonder of creative wisdom, nor even at this time to stress the seventh day as a day of rest. When the story of Moses bringing his people out of Egypt is told young children, the providence of God will be made evident, but the facts of the story itself and its enjoyment just as a story should not in early childhood be overshadowed by attempting to force the moral and religious applications too closely.

It even happens that the indirect lesson, in which the child is left to see for himself the application and meaning, is often the most effective to teaching. The same principle holds when, later in the course, the youth is first studying in its entirety the life of Jesus. The main thing is to get a sympathetic, reverent, connected view of Jesus's life as a whole. There will, of course, be a thousand lessons to be learned and applications to be made from his teachings, but these should rest on a fund of ***accurate information about Jesus himself and what he taught***.

Danger of neglecting information.--It should be clear, then, that in advocating the informational lesson there is no thought of asking that we should teach our children *mere* facts, or fill their heads with *mere* information. The intention is, rather, to stress the important truth often seemingly forgotten, that to be intelligent in one's religion there are certain, fundamental ***things which must be known***; that to be a worthy Christian there are certain facts, stories, personages, and events with a knowledge of which the mind must be well furnished. There can be little doubt that the common run of teaching in our church schools has failed to give our children a ***sufficient basis*** of information upon which to build their religious experience.

Informational instruction may be combined with other types of lessons, or may be given as separate lessons which stress almost entirely the informational aspect of the material. In the younger classes the information will come to the children chiefly in the form of stories, and the accounts of lives of great men and women. Later in the course, Bible narrative, history, and biography will supply the chief sources of informational material.

THE DEVELOPMENTAL LESSON

It is a safe principle in teaching not to give ready-made to children a fact or conclusion which they can easily be led by questions and suggestions to discover for themselves. Truths which one has found out for himself always mean more than matter that is dogmatically forced upon him. The pupil who has watched the bees sucking honey from clover blossoms and then going with pollen-laden feet to another blossom, or one who has observed the drifting pollen from orchard or corn field, is better able to understand the fertilization of plants than he would be from any mere description of the process.

On the same principle, the child will get a deeper and more lasting impression of the effects of disobedience if led to see the effect of the disobedience of Adam and Eve in the shame and sorrow and feeling of guilt that came to them, than he will through listening to ever so many impressive assertions on the sin of disobedience. If the concrete lesson is carried over to his own personal experience and his observation of the results of disobedience, and the unhappiness it has brought, the effect is all the greater.

Purpose of the inductive lesson.--The developmental, or inductive, lesson, therefore, seeks to lead the child to *observe, discover, think, find out for himself*. It begins with concrete and particular instances, but it does not stop with them. It does not at the start force upon the child any rules or general conclusions, but it does seek to arrive at conclusions and rules in the end. For example, the purpose in having the child watch particular bees carrying pollen to blossoms, and in having him observe particular pollen drifting in the wind, is to teach in the end the general truth that *certain plants are dependent on insects and others on currents of air for their pollenization*.

In similar fashion, the purpose in having the child understand the effects of disobedience in the case of Adam and Eve and in any particular instance in his own experience is to teach the general conclusion that *disobedience commonly brings sorrow and trouble*. The aim, then, is to arrive at a universal truth of wide application, but to *reach it through appealing to the child's own knowledge, experience, and observation*. In this way the lesson learned will have more vital meaning and it will be more readily accepted because not forced upon the learner.

Two principles.--Two important principles must be kept in mind in teaching an inductive lesson:

1. A basis or starting point must be found in knowledge or experience already in the learner's possession.

2. The child must have in his mind the question or problem which demands solution.

The first of these principles means that in order for the child to observe, think, discover for himself, he must have a sufficient basis of information from which to proceed. The inductive lesson, therefore, rests upon and starts from the informational lesson. To illustrate, in order to understand and be interested in the work of the bees as pollen-bearers, the child must first ***know the fact*** that the blossoming and fruiting of the common plants depend on pollen. The ear of corn which did not properly fill with grains because something happened to prevent pollen grains from reaching the tips of the silks at the right time, or the apple tree barren because it failed from some adverse cause to receive a supply of pollen for its blossoms may properly be the starting point. The ***problem*** or question then arising is how pollen grains are carried. With this basis of fact and of question, the child is ready to begin the interesting task of observation and discovery under the direction of the teacher; he is then ready for the inductive lesson, in which he will discover new knowledge by using the information already in his mind.

Conducting the inductive lesson.--In conducting the inductive lesson the teacher must from the beginning have a very clear idea of the goal or conclusion to be reached by the learners. Suppose the purpose is to impress on the children the fact of Jesus's love and care for children. The lesson might start with questions and illustrations dealing with the father's and mother's care and love for each child in the home, and the way these are shown.

Following this would come the story of Jesus rebuking his disciples for trying to send the children away, and his own kindness to the children. Then such questions as these: How did the disciples feel about having the children around Jesus? Why did they tell the children to keep away? Perhaps they were afraid the children would annoy or trouble Jesus. Have you ever known anyone who did not seem to like to have children around him? Does your mother like to have you come and be beside her? What did Jesus say about letting the children come to him? Why do you think Jesus liked to have the children around him? How did Jesus show his love for children? Why do you think the children liked to be with Jesus? Do you think that Jesus loves children as much to-day as when he was upon earth? Do you think he wants children to be good and happy now as he did then? In what ways does Jesus show his love and kindness to children? The impression or conclusion to grow out of these questions and the story is that ***Jesus loved and cared for children when he was upon earth, and that he loves and cares for them now just as he did then***. This will be the goal in the teacher's mind from the beginning of the lesson.

THE DEDUCTIVE, OR APPLICATION, LESSON

Not all teaching can be of the inductive, or discovery, type. It is necessary now and then to start with general truths, rules, or principles and apply them to concrete individual cases. Rules and maxims once understood are often serviceable in working out new problems. The conclusions reached from a study of one set of circumstances can frequently be used in meeting similar situations another time.

For example, the child learns by a study of particular instances the results of disobedience, and finally arrives at the great general truth that ***disobedience to the laws of nature or of God is followed by punishment and suffering***. This fact becomes to him a rule, a principle, a maxim, which has universal application. Once this is understood and accepted, the child is armed with a weapon against disobedience. With this equipment he can say when he confronts temptation: This means disobedience to God's law and the laws of nature; but ***disobedience to the laws of God and of nature brings punishment and suffering***; therefore if I do this thing, I shall be punished, and shall suffer--I will refrain from doing it.

Making the application.--A large part of our instruction in religion must be of the deductive kind. It is impossible, even if it were desirable, to rediscover and develop inductively out of observation and experience all the great moral and religious laws which should govern the life. Many of these come to us ready-made, the result of the aggregate experience of generations of religious living, or the product of God's revelation to men. Consider, for example, such great generalizations as: "Where your treasure is, there will your heart be also;" "Blessed are the merciful, for they shall obtain mercy"; "No man can serve two masters"; "With what measure ye mete it shall be measured unto you"; "The wages of sin is death."

These are illustrations of the concentrated wisdom of the finest hearts and minds the world has seen, words spoken by Inspiration, but true to the experience of every person. It is our part as teachers to make the great fundamental moral and religious laws which underlie our lives living truths to our pupils. To do this we must not teach such truths as mere abstractions, but show them at work in the lives of men and women and of boys and girls. We must find illustrations, we must make applications, and discover examples of proof and verification.

Teaching that fails from lack of applying truth.--The object, then, of the *inductive* lesson is to lead the learner to *discover* truth; the object of the *deductive* lesson is to lead him to *apply* truth. There can be little doubt that much of our teaching of religion suffers from failure to make immediate and vital application of the truths we teach. When we teach the youth that no man can serve two masters, we should not be satisfied until we have shown him the proof of this truth at work in the everyday experience of men. When we teach him that the wages of sin is death, we must not stop with the mere statement of fact, but lead him to recognize the effects of sin's work in broken lives and ruined careers.

Nor should we confine our proofs and illustrations to examples taken from the Bible, valuable as these are. Too many, perhaps half unconsciously to themselves, carry the impression that religion belongs rather more to Bible times and peoples than to ourselves. Too many assent to the general truth of religion and the demands it puts on our lives, but fail to make a sufficiently immediate and definite application of its requirements to their own round of daily living. Too many think of the divine law as revealed in the Scriptures as having a historical significance rather than a present application. One of the tasks of deductive teaching is to cure this fatal weakness in the study of religion.

THE DRILL LESSON

Teaching religion does not require as large a proportion of drill as many other subjects. This is because the purpose of drill is to make certain matter automatic in the mind, or to train definite acts to a high degree of skill. For example, the child must come to know his multiplication table readily, "without thinking"; he must come to be able to write or spell or count or manipulate the keys of a typewriter without directing his attention to the acts required. Wherever automatic action or ready skill is required, there drill is demanded. Drill provides for the repetition of the mental or physical act until habit has made it second nature and it goes on practically doing itself. There is no way to get a high degree of skill without drill, for the simple reason that the brain requires a certain amount of repeated action before it can carry out the necessary operations without error and without the application of conscious thought.

Drill lessons in the church school.--While the church-school teacher will not require so much use of drill as the day-school teacher, it is highly essential that drill shall not be omitted at points where it is needed. There are some things which the child should learn very thoroughly and completely in his study of religion. He should know a few prayers by heart, so that their words come to him naturally and easily when he desires to use them. He should know the words and music of certain songs and hymns suited to his age. He should learn certain Bible passages of rare beauty, and other sentiments, verses, and poems found outside the Bible. He should come, as a matter of convenience and skill, to know the names and order of the books of the Bible. In some churches he is required to know the catechism. Whatever of such material is to be mastered fully and completely must receive careful drill.

Principles for conducting the drill.--The first step in a successful drill lesson is to **supply a motive** for the drill. This is necessary in order to secure alertness and effort. **Mere** repetition is not drill. Monotonous going over the words of a poem or the list of books of the Bible with wandering or slack attention will fail of results. The learner must be keyed up, and give himself whole-heartedly to the work. Let the child come to feel a real **need** of mastery, and one great motive is supplied. Let him desire the words of the song because he is to sing in the chorus, or desire the words of the poem because he is to take part in a pageant, and there will be little trouble about willingness to drill.

Again, the competitive impulse can often be used to motivate drill. The child is ambitious to stand at the head of his class, or to beat his own record of performance, or to win the appreciation or praise of teacher or parents, or he has a pride in personal achievement--these are all worthy motives, and can be made of great service in conducting classroom or individual drills. The posting of a piece of good work done by a pupil, or calling attention to the good performance of a member of the class can often be made an incentive to the whole number.

Drill, in order to be effective, must not stop short of thorough mastery. The matter which is barely learned, or the verse which can be but doubtfully repeated is sure to escape if not fixed by further drill. It is probable, as suggested in an earlier chapter, that we attempt to have our children memorize too much Bible material which is beyond their understanding and too difficult for them. On the other hand, there can be no doubt that we fail to teach them sufficiently well the smaller amount of beautiful sentiments, verses, poems, songs, and prayers which should be a part of the mental and spiritual possession of every child. Our weekly lessons provide for the memorizing of Bible matter week by week, yet surprisingly few children can repeat any sensible amount of such material. Better results would follow if we should require less material, select it more wisely, and then **drill upon it until it is firmly fixed in the mind as a permanent and familiar possession**.

THE APPRECIATION LESSON

It is quite as essential that the child shall come to enjoy and admire right things as that he shall know right things. To cultivate appreciation for the beautiful, the good, the fine, and the true is one of the great aims of our teaching. One who is able to analyze a flower and technically describe its botanical parts, but who fails to respond to its beauty has still much to learn about flowers. One who learns the facts about the life of Paul, Elijah, or Jesus but who does not feel and admire the strength, gentleness, and goodness of their characters has missed one of the essential points in his study. One who masters the details about a poem or a picture but who misses the thrill of enjoyment and appreciation which it holds for him has gathered but the husks and misses the right kernel of meaning.

How to teach appreciation.--Appreciation can never be taught directly. The best we can do is to bring to the child the thing of beauty or goodness which we desire him to enjoy and admire, making sure that he comprehends its meaning as fully as may be, and then leave it to exert its own appeal. We may by ill-advised comment or insistence even hinder appreciation. The teacher who constantly asks the children, "Do you not think the poem is beautiful?" or, "Is not this a lovely song?" not only fails to help toward appreciation, but is in danger of creating a false attitude in the child by causing him to express admiration where none is felt.

There is also grave doubt whether it is not a mistake to urge too much on the child that he "ought" to love God, or that it is his "duty" to love the church. The fact is that love, admiration and appreciation ***cannot be compelled*** by any act of the will or sense of duty. They must arise spontaneously from a realization of some lovable or beautiful quality which exerts an appeal that will not be denied.

The part of the teacher at this point, therefore, is to act as interpreter, to help the learner to grasp the meaning of the poem, the picture, the song, or the character he is studying. The admirable qualities are to be brought out, the beautiful aspects set forth, and the lovable traits placed in high light. The teacher may even express his own admiration and appreciation, though without sentimentality or effusiveness. Nor is it likely that a teacher will be able to excite admiration in his class for any object of study which he does not himself admire. If his own soul does not rise to the beauty of the twenty-third psalm or to the inimitable grandeur and strength of the Christ-life, he is hardly the one to hold these subjects of study before children.

THE REVIEW LESSON

Reviews and tests fulfill a double purpose for the learner: they help to organize and make more usable the matter that has been learned, and they reveal success or failure in mastery. They also serve the teacher as a measure of his success in teaching. The review lesson should not be, as it often is, a mere repetition of as many facts from, previous lessons as time will permit to be covered. It should present a ***new view*** of the subject. It should deal with the great essential points, and so relate and organize them that the threefold aim of ***fruitful knowledge***, ***right attitudes***, and ***practical applications*** shall be stressed and made secure.

Guiding principles.--If the section of matter under review deals with a series of events, such as the story of the migration of the Israelites from Egypt or the account of the ministry of Jesus, then the review lesson must pick out and emphasize those incidents and applications which should become a part of the permanent possession of the child's mind from the study of this material. These related points should be so linked together and so reimpressed that they will form a continuous view of the period or topic studied. There is no place for the incidental nor for minute and unrelated detail in the review.

The teacher will need most careful preparation and planning to conduct a review. He must have the entire field to be reviewed fully mastered and in his own mind as a unit, else he cannot lead the child back over it successfully. He must work out a lesson plan which will secure interest and response on the part of his pupils. Many review lessons drag, and are but endured by the class. This may be accounted for by the fact that the review recitation often fails to do more than repeat old material. It may also come from the fact that the children are asked details which they have forgotten or never knew, so that they are unable to take their part. It may in some cases arise from the fact that the teacher is himself not ready for the review, and does not like review days. Whatever may be the cause, the review that fails to catch interest or call forth enthusiasm has in so far failed of its purpose. The minds of teacher and pupils should be at their best and concentration at its keenest for the review lesson.

ASSIGNMENT OF LESSON

No small part of the success of instruction depends on faithfulness and skill in assigning lessons. Too often this is left for the very last moment of the class hour, when there is no time left for proper assignment and the teacher can give only the most hurried and incomplete directions. Or, it may be that the only direction that is given is the exhortation to "be sure to prepare the lesson for next week." But this will not suffice. We must not forget that children, especially the younger children, may not know just how to go to work upon the lesson, nor what to do in getting it. It is hard for any young child to gather thought from the printed page, even after he has attained fair skill in reading; and it is doubly hard if the matter is difficult or unfamiliar, as is much of the material found in the church-school lessons.

How to make the assignment.--In order to assign the lesson properly the teacher must, of course, be perfectly familiar with the coming lesson. This means that he must keep a week ahead in his preparation, which is in the end no loss, but even a gain. The teacher must also have the plan of the lesson sufficiently in mind that he knows just what points are to be stressed, what will present the most difficulty to the class, what will most appeal to their interest, and what will need to be especially assigned for study or investigation. In lessons which children are to prepare at home it is usually well to go over the material briefly with the class in making the assignment, giving hints for study, calling attention to interesting points, and stating very definitely just what the class is expected to do.

If there is to be written work, this should be fully understood: if handwork or drawing or coloring, it should be made perfectly clear what is required; if memory material is asked for, it should be gone over, the meaning made clear to every child, and directions given as to how best to commit the matter. If outside references are assigned in books or magazines, the reference should be written down in the notebook or given the child on a slip of paper so that no mistake may be made. The purpose and requirement in all these matters is to be as definite and clear as would be required in any business concern, leaving no chance for failure or mistake because of lack of understanding. Less than this is an evidence of carelessness or incompetence in the teacher.

1. In order better to understand and to review the several types of lessons listed in the chapter it will be well for you to look through the lessons for the current quarter or year and determine to which type each separate lesson belongs. How many do you find of each type? Are there many lessons that will involve several of the types?

2. Which type of these lessons do you best like to teach? Is there any particular type that you have been neglecting? Any in which you feel that you are not very successful? What will you need to do to increase your efficiency on this type of lesson?

3. Do you feel that you are reasonably skillful in leading children to discover truths for themselves through the use of questions? If you find when questioning that the children lack the information necessary to arriving at the truth desired, what must you then do? What do you consider your greatest weakness in conducting the developmental lesson?

4. Does your class like review lessons? If not, can you discover the reason? Have your reviews been largely repetitions of matter already covered, or have they used such devices as to bring the matter up in new guise? Do you believe that review day can be made the most interesting of the lessons? Some teachers say it can, How will you go at it to make it so?

5. What application, or deductive, lesson have you taught your class recently? Was it a success? Have you ever discovered a tendency in your teaching to have your class commit to memory some great truth, but fail in its application to real problems in their own lives? What applications of religious truths have you recently

made successfully in your class?

6. What is your method or plan of assigning lessons? Do you think that any part of the children's failure to prepare their lessons may be due to imperfect assignments? Will you make the assignment of the lessons that lie ahead one of your chief problems?

FOR FURTHER READING
Earhart, Types of Teaching.
Strayer, A Brief Course in the Teaching Process.
Hayward, The Lesson in Appreciation.
Knight, Some Principles of Teaching as Applied to the Sunday School.
Maxwell, The Observation of Teaching.

CHAPTER XII
METHODS USED IN THE RECITATION

The particular mode of procedure used in recitation will depend on the nature of the material, the age of the pupils, and the aim of the lesson. For the church-school recitation period four different methods are chiefly used. These are:

1. The *topical* method, in which the teacher suggests a topic of the lesson or asks a question and requires the pupil to go on in his own way and tell what he can about the point under discussion.

2. The *lecture* method, in which the teacher himself discusses the topic of the lesson, presenting the facts, offering explanations or making applications as he judges the case may require.

3. The *question-and-answer*, or discussion, method, in which the teacher leads in a half-formal conversation, asking questions and receiving answers either to test the pupil's preparation or to develop the facts and meanings of the lesson.

4. The *story* method, in which the teacher uses a story, told either in the words of the writer or in his own words, to convey the lesson. The story method differs from the lecture method in that the story recounts some real or fancied situation or occurrence to convey the lesson, while the lecture depends more on explanation and analysis.

It may sometimes happen that an entire recitation will employ but one of these methods, the whole time being given either to reciting upon topics, to a lecture or discussion by the teacher, or to a series of questions and answers. More commonly, however, the three methods are best when combined to supplement each other or to give variety to the instruction.

THE TOPICAL METHOD

There is really no absolute line of demarkation between the topical and the question-and-answer method. The chief difference lies in the fact that the *question* deals with some one specific fact or point, while the *topic* requires the pupil to decide on what facts or points should come into the discussion, and, so make his own plan for the discussion.

The plan of the topical method.--It is evident that the topical method of reciting will require more independence of thought than the question-and-answer method. To ask the child to "give the account of Noah's building of the Ark," or to "tell about Joseph being sold by his brothers" is to demand more of him than to answer a series of questions on, these events. The topical method will, therefore, find its greatest usefulness in the higher grades rather than with the younger children. This does not mean, however, that children in the earlier grades are to be given no opportunity to formulate their thought for themselves and to express their thought without the help of direct questions.

This power, like all others, is developed through its use, and is not acquired at a certain age without practice. Even young children may be encouraged to retell stories in their own words, or to tell what they think about any problem that interests them; and all such exercises are the best of preliminary training in the use of the topical method.

Narrative topics.--The easiest form of the topical method is that dealing with *narration*. Children are much more adept at telling *what happened*--recounting a series of events in a game, a trip, an incident, or an accident--than in giving a *description* of persons, places, or objects. The Bible narratives will therefore afford good starting places for topical recitations in the younger grades. Older pupils may be called upon to discuss problems of conduct, or to make applications of lessons to concrete conditions, or carry on any other form of analysis that calls for individual thought and ability in expression.

Report topics.--A modified form of the topical method is sometimes called the *report* method, or the *research* method. In this use of the topical method some special and definite topic or problem is assigned a pupil to be prepared by special study, and reported upon before the class. This plan, at least above the elementary grades, has great possibilities if wisely used. The topics, if interesting, and if adapted to the children, will usually receive careful preparation. Especially is this true if well-prepared pupils are allowed in the recitation to make a brief report to an interested audience of classmates.

Care must be taken in the use of this method not to permit the time of the class to be taken with uninteresting and poorly prepared reports by pupils, for this will kill the interest of the class, set a low standard of preparation and mastery, and render the method useless. When a topic of special study is assigned to a pupil, care must be taken to see that the exact references for study are known and that the necessary material is available. The devoted teacher will also try to find time and opportunity to help his pupil organize the material of his report to insure its interest and value to the class.

Avoiding a danger.--A danger to be avoided in the use of the topical method is that of accepting incomplete and unenlightening discussions from pupils who are poorly prepared. To say to a child, "Tell what you can about David and Goliath," and then to pass on to something else after a poorly given account of the interesting story is to fail in the best use of the topical method. After the child has finished his recitation the teacher should then supplement with facts or suggestions, or ask questions to bring out further information, or do whatever else is necessary to enrich and make more vivid the impression gained. This must all be done, however, without making an earnest child feel that his effort has been useless, or that what he has given, was unimportant.

THE LECTURE METHOD

The lecture method, if followed continuously, is a poor way of teaching. Even in telling stories to the younger children, the skillful teacher leads the pupils to tell the stories back to her and the class. Mere listening gets to be dull work, and the teacher who does all the reciting himself must expect lack of interest and inattention.

There can be no doubt that many teachers talk too much themselves compared with the part taken by their pupils. It is much easier for the teacher to go over the lesson himself, bringing out its incidents, explaining its meanings, and applying its lessons, than to lead the class, by means of well-directed questions, to accomplish these things by their own answers and discussions. Yet it is a common experience, especially with children, that we like best any program, recitation, or exercise, in which we ourselves have had an active part. And it is also from the lesson in which we have really participated that we carry away the most vivid and lasting impressions.

The lecture method not for general use.--Every teacher should therefore consider, when making his lesson plan, just what his own part is to be in the presentation of material. Some latitude must be allowed, of course, for circumstances which may arise in the recitation bringing up points which may need elaboration or explanation. But he should know in a general way what material he is to bring in, what applications he will emphasize, and what illustrations he will use. He should not trust to the inspiration of the moment, nor allow himself to be led off into a discussion that monopolizes all the time and deprives the class of participation. More than one church-school class has failed to hold the interest, if not the attendance, of its members because the teacher mistook his function and formed the habit of turning expositor or preacher before his class. The overtalkative teacher should learn to curb this tendency, or else give way to one who brings less of himself and more of his pupils to bear upon the lesson.

This does not mean that the teacher shall never lecture or talk to his class. Indeed, the teacher who does not have a message now and then for his pupils is not qualified to guide their spiritual development. It means, rather, that lecturing must not become a habit, and that on the whole it should be used sparingly with all classes of children. It means also that all matter presented to the class by the teacher himself should be well prepared; that it should be carefully organized and planned, so that its meaning will be clear and its lesson plain, and so that time will not be wasted in its presentation. It will be a safe rule for the teacher to set for himself not to come before his class with a talk that is not as well prepared as he expects his minister to have his sermon. And why not! The recitation hour should mean at least as much to the church class as the sermon hour means to the congregation.

THE QUESTION-AND-ANSWER METHOD

Skill in questioning lies at the basis of most good teaching of children. Good questioning stimulates thought, brings out new meanings, and leads the mind to right conclusions. Poor questioning leaves the thought unawakened, fails to arouse interest and attention, and results in poor mastery and faulty understanding. To the uninitiated it appears easy to ask questions for others to answer. But when we become teachers and undertake to use the question as an instrument of instruction we find that it is much harder to ask questions than to answer them, for not only must the questioner know the subject and the answer to each question better than his pupils, but he must be able constantly to interpret the minds of his pupils in order to discover their understanding of the problem and to know what questions next to ask.

Questions slavishly dependent on the text.--Not infrequently one finds a teacher who uses questioning solely to test the knowledge of the pupils on the lesson text. Probably the worst form of this kind of questioning is that of following the printed questions of the lesson quarterly, the pupils having their lesson sheets open before them and looking up the answer to each question as it is asked.

The following questions are taken from a widely used junior quarterly, the Bible text being Luke 10. 25-37: "Who wanted to try Jesus? What did he ask? What did Jesus say? What reply was made? What questions did the lawyer ask? How did Jesus answer him? What is such a story called? What is the name of this parable? Where was the man going? Who met him? How did they treat him? What did they take from him? Where did they leave him?" No one of these questions appeals to thought or imagination. All are questions of sheer fact, with none of the deeper and more interesting meanings brought. All of them may be answered correctly, and the child be little the wiser religiously. Such a method of teaching cannot do other than deaden the child's interest in the Bible, create in him an aversion to the lesson hour of the church school, and fail of the whole purpose of religious education. The teacher must *be able to use living questions, and not be dependent on a dead list of faulty questions embalmed in print*.

Questions arising spontaneously from the topic.--One who does not know his lesson well enough so that he can ask the necessary questions practically without reference even to the text, let alone referring to the printed questions, or asking questions in the words of the text, is not yet ready to teach the lesson. In order to successful teaching there must be a constant interchange of response between teacher and class at every moment throughout the recitation. This is impossible if the teacher must stop to read the text of the lesson, or take her eyes and attention away from the class to look up the question which is to come next. All such breaks of thought are fatal to interest and attention on the part of the class.

As suggested in an earlier chapter, the teacher should have prepared a list of pivotal questions as a part of her lesson plan. With these at hand there should be no necessity for reference to the printed lesson to find questions during the recitation period. Let the teacher who is accustomed to slavish dependence on the lesson text for his questions really master his lesson, and then declare his independence of tread-mill questioning; he will be surprised at the added satisfaction and efficiency that come to his teaching.

The principle of unity.--Questions that really teach must follow some plan of *unity* or continuity. Each succeeding question must grow out of the preceding question and its answer, and all put together must lead in a definite direction toward a clear aim or goal which the teacher has in mind. One of the serious faults of the questions quoted above from the lesson quarterly is that they lack unity and purpose. Each question is separate from all the others. No question leads to the ones which follow, nor does the whole list point to any lesson or conclusion at the end. Such questioning can result only in isolated scraps of information. A series of questions lacking unity and purpose resembles a broom ending in many straws, instead of being like a bayonet ending in a point: and who would not prefer a bayonet to a broom as a weapon of offense!

The principle of clearness.--The good questioner makes his questions *clear and definite* so that they can not be misunderstood. That this is not always accomplished is proved by the fact that a child who is unable to answer a question when it is put in one form may answer it perfectly when it is asked in different phrasing. The teacher always needs to make certain that the question is fully comprehended, for it is evident that an answer cannot exceed the understanding of the question in clearness.

To be clear, a question must be free from obscure wording. One primary teacher, seeking to show how each animal is adapted to the life it must live, asked the class, "Why has a cat fur and a duck feathers?" Just what did she mean for the child to answer? Did she mean to inquire why a cat has fur instead of feathers, and a duck feathers instead of fur, or did she mean to ask why each has its own particular coating regardless of the other? Another teacher asked, "Why did Jesus's parents go up to Jerusalem when Jesus was twelve years old?" Did he mean to ask why they went when Jesus was just at this age, or did he mean to ask why they went at all, the age of Jesus being incidental? One can only guess at his meaning, hence the answer could at best be but a guess.

Questions to be within the learner's grasp.--If questions are to be clear to the child they must deal with matter within his grasp. These questions are taken from an *intermediate* quarterly: "Why was the New Testament written? What was the purpose of the book of Revelation? Fit the epistle of Paul into the story of his life. What is meant by inspiration? What are the reasons for calling the Bible the most wonderful book in the world?" These questions are all clear enough so far as their wording is concerned, but they belong to the college or theological seminary age instead of to the intermediate age. While our questions should make our pupils think, they must not go over their heads, for one does not commonly think on a question whose very meaning is beyond his grasp!

Some questions lack definiteness because several correct answers could be given to the question. Here are a few such: What did Paul claim concerning one of his epistles? What did Moses do when he came down from the mountain? What were the priests of the temple required to have? What happened when Jesus was crucified? What of John the Baptist? What about Ruth and Naomi? What did Judas become? No one of these questions asks any definite thing. To answer any of them the pupil must guess at the particular thing the teacher has in mind. Many answers may be given to each question which are as correct and which answer the question as well as the answer the teacher seeks from the pupil. Such questioning comes either from lack of clearness and definiteness in the teacher's thinking, with a consequent uncertainty as what he really does mean to ask, or else from a mental laziness which shrinks from the effort necessary to formulate the question definitely.

Questions should stimulate thought.--Questions should be thought-provoking. Usually it is a mistake to ask questions that can be answered, by a simple *Yes* or *No*, though there are occasions when this may be done. For example, children will not be required to think when asked such questions as, Was Moses leader of the Israelites? or Did Jesus want his disciples to keep children away from him? But they will require thought to answer Yes or No to such questions as, Should Esther have asked that Haman be hanged? or, Can God forgive us for a wrong act if we are not penitent?

Leading questions, or questions that suggest the answer, do not encourage thought. To ask, Do you not think that God is pained when we do wrong? or What ought you to say in return when some one has done you a favor? is to leave the child himself too little to do in answering. The *alternative* question, or the question that simply allows the choice between two suggested possibilities is also fruitless so far as demanding thought is concerned. In a question like, Was Paul a Gentile or was he a Jew? the bright child can usually tell from the teacher's inflection how to answer. In any case he will run an even chance of giving the right answer from sheer guessing.

The order of questioning.--It is a mistake to ask questions in serial order, so that each child knows just when he is to be called upon. This method invites carelessness and inattention. There should be no set order, nor should a child who has just been called upon feel that he is now safe from further questioning. The element of uncertainty as to when the next question will come is a good incentive to alertness. The pupil who shows signs of mischief or inattention may well become the immediate mark for a question, and thereby be tided past the danger point.

Usually the question should be addressed to the entire class, and then a pause of a few seconds ensue before the one who is to answer is designated. Care must be taken, however, not to wait too long between asking the question and calling the name of the one expected to answer, for attention and curiosity quickly fall away, and time and interest are lost and the recitation becomes slow.

The reception of answers.--The teacher's reception of the child's answer is almost as important as the manner of asking the question. First of all, the teacher must be interested in the answer. This interest must be real, and must show in the manner. Not to look into the eyes of the child who is answering is to fail to pay the courtesy due one who is conversing with us; it is not only bad manners but worse pedagogy. The interested, sympathetic eye of the teacher has a wonderful power of encouragement and stimulus to the child, while an attitude of indifference on the part of the teacher is at once fatal to his enthusiasm. One of the besetting sins of many teachers is to repeat the pupils' answers after them. This habit probably has its rise in mental unreadiness on the part of the teacher, who repeats what the child has just said while getting ready to ask the next question. Besides being a great waste of time, the repeating of answers is discourteous, and is a source of distraction, and annoyance to pupils.

Finally, we may say that good questioning on the part of the teacher leads to questions on the part of the pupils. The relations between teacher and class always should be such, that the children, feel free to ask questions on any points of the lesson, and they should be encouraged to do so. The teacher must have the tact and skill, however, not to be led away from the topic by irrelevant questions nor to be required to waste time by discussing unimportant points which may be brought in. It is to be feared that valuable time is sometimes lost in adult classes in discussing controversial questions that ought not to have been asked.

THE STORY METHOD

The use of the story method of instruction has been mentioned many times in the course of our discussion. It will still be worth while, however, to note a few of the principles upon which the successful telling of stories depends.

First of all, a story is--just a story! It is not an argument, nor an explanation, not a description, nor a lecture in disguise. A story is a narrative of a series of events, which may be either real or imaginary. These events are so related as to form a closely connected unity from beginning to end, and they are of such nature as to appeal to imagination, interest, and emotion more than to the intellect. The successful handling of the story depends on two chief factors: (1) *the plan or arrangement* of the story itself, and (2) skill in telling the story.

The story itself.--The story must not be too long, or interest will weaken and attention will flag. It must have an interesting beginning, so that attention and anticipation are aroused from the very first sentence. "Once upon a time..." "A long time ago when the fairies..." "There once lived a king who..."--these all contain a hint of mystery or of interesting possibilities certain to invite response from children. The commonplace beginning is illustrated in a story in a primary leaflet which starts, "There was once a mother, who loved her child as all mothers do." There is no invitation here to imagination or anticipation, and the evident attempt to enforce a moral truth in the opening sentence detracts from its effectiveness.

The major characters of the story should be introduced in the opening sentences. The story should possess a close-knit unity, and not admit incidental or supplemental characters or events that play no direct part in the sequel. It must be so planned as to proceed to a *climax*, and this climax should be reached without unnecessary deviations and wanderings. We all know that type of story in which the main point is all but lost in a multiplicity of unnecessary details. On the other hand, points necessary to the climax must not be omitted. The climax may be the end of the story, or an ending may be provided following the climax. In either case the ending should leave the mind of the listener at rest as to the outcome. That is to say, there should remain no mystery or uncertainty or unpleasant feeling of incompleteness. The ending of a story should be as carefully phrased as its beginning. Even if the story has a sad ending, which is usually not best in children's stories, it should have some element in it which makes such a conclusion inevitable, and so leaves the mind in a sense satisfied.

Guiding principles.--The rules to guide in planning the story itself may, then, be stated as follows:

1. Decide on the *truth to be conveyed*, and make the story lead up to this.

2. Use great care to compel interest and anticipation through an *effective beginning*.

3. Plan to have the body of the story reasonably brief, and to make the main truth *stand out in a climax*. Eliminate all complications or irrelevant matter that does not aid in leading up to the climax. Elaborate and stress all features that help in making the impression to be attained in the climax.

4. Make the ending such as to leave in the mind a feeling that the story was *satisfactory and complete*.

Telling the story.--The effective story must be *told*. It cannot be read without losing something of spontaneity and attractiveness. It cannot even be committed to memory and repeated; for here also is lacking something of the living glow and appeal that come from having the words spring fresh and warm from the mind that is actually thinking and feeling them. Most story-tellers find that it pays to work out carefully and commit to memory the opening and closing sentences of a story; the phrasing is so important here that it should not be left to chance. But the body of the story is better given extemporaneously even if the wording is not as perfect as it could be made by reading or reciting the matter.

Before trying to tell a story before his class, the teacher should rehearse it several times. Nothing but practice will give the ease, certainty, and spontaneity necessary to good story-telling. Even professional story-tellers realize that they do not tell a new story well until they have told it a number of times. Perhaps this is in part because one never enjoys telling a story until he is sure he can tell it well, and so get a response from his listeners. And one never tells a story really well unless he himself enjoys both the story and its telling. One never brings the full effectiveness of a story to bear on his hearers unless he himself enters fully into its appreciation, and moves himself while stirring the emotions of those who listen.

The right atmosphere required.--Second in importance only to preparing himself for the telling of the story is the preparing of the class to listen. The right atmosphere of thought, attitude and feeling should be created for the story before it is begun. A primary teacher was about to begin a story whose purpose was to show how God cares for the birds by giving them feathers to keep them warm, wings for swift flying, and cozy nests for their homes, when suddenly a little bird flew in through the classroom window and was killed before the class by dashing against the wall. Of course the right atmosphere for her story was then impossible, and she wisely left it for another time.

The approach to the story can be made by some question or suggestion relating to the pupils' own experience, by a sentence or two of explanation, or by an illustration dealing with matters familiar to the class. But whatever device is used, the introduction should prepare the minds of the class to receive the story by turning their thought in the direction which the story is to take. It is also important that any new terms or unfamiliar situations which are to be used in the story, and which might not be understood by the class, shall be cleared up before the story is begun.

Arts and devices of the story-teller.--The skillful story-teller will soon learn to use certain arts and devices to make the telling more effective. One such device is the use of direct discourse; that is, instead of telling *about* the giants, the fairies, the animals, give them human speech and let them speak for themselves, like the bear in Little Red Riding Hood. Another effective device is that of repeating in the course of the story certain important words or phrases until from this repetition they stand out and become emphasized. Some of the best story-tellers make effective use of pauses, thus creating a situation of curiosity and suspense in the minds of the listeners. The pause must be neither too long nor too short, nor can any tell just how long it ought to be except from the response of the children themselves, which the teacher must be able to sense accurately and unfailingly. Much may be added to the effect of stories by skillful use of the various arts of expression, such as facial expression, voice tone, quality, and inflection, and gesture. The use of mimicry, imitation, and impersonation is also very effective if this ability comes naturally to the one who attempts to use it, but these would better be omitted than poorly done.

Good stories sometimes lose much of their effectiveness by having the moral stated at the end, or by having an attempt at moralizing too evident in the telling of the story. A story which has a lesson inherent in the story itself will teach its own moral if it is well told. If the truth to be conveyed is not clear to the child from the story, it will hardly appeal to him by having it tacked on at the end.

*　　*　　*　　*　　*

We have, then, come to the end of our brief study of the teaching of religion. We have seen some of its principles and methods, and have discovered these at work in various illustrations and applications. It now remains to realize that these are all to be found in brief epitome in the work of the Great Teacher. For Jesus was first of all a *teacher*, rather than a preacher. And as a teacher he supplied the model which anticipated all modern psychology and scientific pedagogy, and gave us in his concrete example and method a standard which the most skillful among us never wholly attain. While we may love Jesus as a friend, come to him as a comforter and helper, seek to follow him as a guide, and worship him as a Saviour, it will be well for us now and then momentarily to place these relations in the background and study him just as a ***teacher***.

Jesus possessed an attractive, inspiring, compelling personality. People naturally came to him with their questions and problems. His quick sympathy, ready understanding, and unerring insight invited friendship, confidence, and devotion. He was ever sure of his "great objective," and whether he was teaching his disciples stupendous truths about the kingdom of God, or whether he was pointing the wayward woman the way to a reconstructed life, the welfare of the ***living soul before him*** was his controlling thought. Jesus had a true sense of the value of a life, and no life was too humble or too unpromising for him to lavish upon it all the wealth of his interest and all the power of his sympathy and helpfulness. He did not feel that his time was poorly spent when he was teaching small groups, and many of the choicest gems of his teaching were given to a mere handful of earnest listeners seated at his feet.

In all his teaching Jesus manifested a deep reverence for vital ***truth***. He told his disciples, "The truth shall make you free." He was never afraid of truth, but accepted it reverently, even when it ran counter to accepted authority. Nor did Jesus ever lose time or opportunity in teaching trivial and unessential matters to his hearers; the knowledge he gave them was always of such fruitful nature that they could at once apply it to their living. Jesus's teaching carried over; it showed its effect in changed attitudes of life, in new purposes, compelling ideals, and great loyalties and devotions. Out of a band of commonplace fishermen and ordinary men he made a company of evangelists and reformers whose work and influence changed the course of civilization. Every person who responded to his instruction felt the glow of a new ambition and the desire to have a part in the great mission. Thus the teaching of Jesus entered into the actual life and conduct of his pupils. The truths he taught did not lie dormant as so much mere attainment of knowledge. They took root and blossomed into action, into transformed lives, and into heroic deeds of kindly service. The constant keynote and demand of Jesus's teaching was shown forth in his, "He that heareth these sayings of mine and doeth them"; he was never satisfied without the doing.

Much is to be learned from the technique of Jesus's teaching, imperfect though the account is of his instruction. He always met his hearers on the plane of their own lives. He would begin his instruction with some common and familiar experience, and lead by questions or illustrations to the truth he wished to present. In this way, without the use of technical words or long phrases, he was able to teach deep and significant truths even to relatively uninformed minds. Jesus appealed to the imagination through picturesque illustrations and parables. He made his hearers think for the truth they reached, and so presented each truth that its application to some immediate problem or need could not be escaped. He was always interesting in his lessons, for they did not deal with unimportant matters nor with tiresome platitudes. He never failed to have definite aim or conclusion toward which his teaching was directed, and the words or questions he used in his instruction moved without deviation toward the accomplishment of this aim. He was too clear, too deeply in earnest, and too completely the master of what he was teaching ever to wander, or be uncertain or to waste time and opportunity. He felt too compelling a love for those he taught ever to fail at his task.

Finally, Jesus was himself the embodiment of the truths and ideals he offered others. He lived the lessons he desired his pupils to learn. He rendered concrete in himself the religion he would have his followers adopt. His life was a lesson which all could learn and follow.

1. Which type of recitation method do you most commonly employ? Which do you like best? Do you combine the several methods occasionally in the same recitation? Do you plan which is best for each particular occasion?

2. To what extent do you use the topical method? Do your pupils succeed in discussing the topics with fair completeness? Do you always supplement with matter of your own, or expand the topics by asking questions when the discussion has been incomplete?

3. Stenographic reports of various recitations have shown that teachers often themselves use from two to three or four times as many words in the lesson hour as all the pupils combined. Do you believe that for young pupils this is good teaching? Have you any accurate notion of the time you yourself take? Do you talk too

much?

4. Study your questioning in the recitation and determine as well as you can which of the principles of good questioning you are most successful in applying; which you are least successful in applying.

5. To what extent do you use the story as a method of instruction? How do you judge you would rank as a story-teller? To what extent have you studied the art of story-telling? Are you constantly improving? What difference have you noted in the interest of a class when a story is ***told*** and when it is ***read***?

FOR FURTHER READING
Betts, The Recitation.
Hamilton, The Recitation.
Home, Story-Telling, Questioning and Studying.
St. John, Stories and Story-Telling.
Houghton, Telling Bible Stories.

The Codes Of Hammurabi And Moses
W. W. Davies

The discovery of the Hammurabi Code is one of the greatest achievements of archaeology, and is of paramount interest, not only to the student of the Bible, but also to all those interested in ancient history...

Religion   **ISBN:** *1-59462-338-4*

QTY

Pages:132
MSRP $12.95

The Theory of Moral Sentiments
Adam Smith

This work from 1749. contains original theories of conscience amd moral judgment and it is the foundation for systemof morals.

Philosophy **ISBN:** *1-59462-777-0*

QTY

Pages:536
MSRP $19.95

Jessica's First Prayer
Hesba Stretton

In a screened and secluded corner of one of the many railway-bridges which span the streets of London there could be seen a few years ago, from five o'clock every morning until half past eight, a tidily set-out coffee-stall, consisting of a trestle and board, upon which stood two large tin cans, with a small fire of charcoal burning under each so as to keep the coffee boiling during the early hours of the morning when the work-people were thronging into the city on their way to their daily toil...

QTY

Pages:84

Childrens   **ISBN:** *1-59462-373-2*

MSRP $9.95

My Life and Work
Henry Ford

Henry Ford revolutionized the world with his implementation of mass production for the Model T automobile. Gain valuable business insight into his life and work with his own auto-biography... "We have only started on our development of our country we have not as yet, with all our talk of wonderful progress, done more than scratch the surface. The progress has been wonderful enough but..."

QTY

Pages:300

Biographies/   **ISBN:** *1-59462-198-5*

MSRP $21.95

The Art of Cross-Examination
Francis Wellman

QTY

I presume it is the experience of every author, after his first book is published upon an important subject, to be almost overwhelmed with a wealth of ideas and illustrations which could readily have been included in his book, and which to his own mind, at least, seem to make a second edition inevitable. Such certainly was the case with me; and when the first edition had reached its sixth impression in five months, I rejoiced to learn that it seemed to my publishers that the book had met with a sufficiently favorable reception to justify a second and considerably enlarged edition. ..

Reference   **ISBN: *1-59462-647-2***

Pages:412
MSRP $19.95

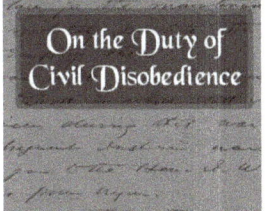

On the Duty of Civil Disobedience
Henry David Thoreau

QTY

Thoreau wrote his famous essay, On the Duty of Civil Disobedience, as a protest against an unjust but popular war and the immoral but popular institution of slave-owning. He did more than write—he declined to pay his taxes, and was hauled off to gaol in consequence. Who can say how much this refusal of his hastened the end of the war and of slavery ?

Law   **ISBN: *1-59462-747-9***

Pages:48
MSRP $7.45

Dream Psychology
Psychoanalysis for Beginners

Sigmund Freud

Dream Psychology Psychoanalysis for Beginners
Sigmund Freud

QTY

Sigmund Freud, born Sigismund Schlomo Freud (May 6, 1856 - September 23, 1939), was a Jewish-Austrian neurologist and psychiatrist who co-founded the psychoanalytic school of psychology. Freud is best known for his theories of the unconscious mind, especially involving the mechanism of repression; his redefinition of sexual desire as mobile and directed towards a wide variety of objects; and his therapeutic techniques, especially his understanding of transference in the therapeutic relationship and the presumed value of dreams as sources of insight into unconscious desires.

Psychology   **ISBN: *1-59462-905-6***

Pages:196
MSRP $15.45

The Miracle of Right Thought
Orison Swett Marden

QTY

Believe with all of your heart that you will do what you were made to do. When the mind has once formed the habit of holding cheerful, happy, prosperous pictures, it will not be easy to form the opposite habit. It does not matter how improbable or how far away this realization may see, or how dark the prospects may be, if we visualize them as best we can, as vividly as possible, hold tenaciously to them and vigorously struggle to attain them, they will gradually become actualized, realized in the life. But a desire, a longing without endeavor, a yearning abandoned or held indifferently will vanish without realization.

Self Help   **ISBN: *1-59462-644-8***

Pages:360
MSRP $25.45

QTY

☐ **The Rosicrucian Cosmo-Conception Mystic Christianity** *by Max Heindel*　ISBN: 1-59462-188-8　**$38.95**
The Rosicrucian Cosmo-conception is not dogmatic, neither does it appeal to any other authority than the reason of the student. It is: not controversial, but is: sent forth in the, hope that it may help to clear...　　New Age/Religion Pages 646

☐ **Abandonment To Divine Providence** *by Jean-Pierre de Caussade*　ISBN: 1-59462-228-0　**$25.95**
"The Rev. Jean Pierre de Caussade was one of the most remarkable spiritual writers of the Society of Jesus in France in the 18th Century. His death took place at Toulouse in 1751. His works have gone through many editions and have been republished...　Inspirational/Religion Pages 400

☐ **Mental Chemistry** *by Charles Haanel*　ISBN: 1-59462-192-6　**$23.95**
Mental Chemistry allows the change of material conditions by combining and appropriately utilizing the power of the mind. Much like applied chemistry creates something new and unique out of careful combinations of chemicals the mastery of mental chemistry...　New Age/Business Pages 354

☐ **The Letters of Robert Browning and Elizabeth Barret Barrett 1845-1846 vol II**　ISBN: 1-59462-193-4　**$35.95**
by Robert Browning and Elizabeth Barrett　　Biographies Pages 596

☐ **Gleanings In Genesis (volume I)** *by Arthur W. Pink*　ISBN: 1-59462-130-6　**$27.45**
Appropriately has Genesis been termed "the seed plot of the Bible" for in it we have, in germ form, almost all of the great doctrines which are afterwards fully developed in the books of Scripture which follow...　Religion/Inspirational Pages 420

☐ **The Master Key** *by L. W. de Laurence*　ISBN: 1-59462-001-6　**$30.95**
In no branch of human knowledge has there been a more lively increase of the spirit of research during the past few years than in the study of Psychology, Concentration and Mental Discipline. The requests for authentic lessons in Thought Control, Mental Discipline and...　New Age/Science Pages 422

☐ **The Lesser Key Of Solomon Goetia** *by L. W. de Laurence*　ISBN: 1-59462-092-X　**$9.95**
This translation of the first book of the "Lemegton" which is now for the first time made accessible to students of Talismanic Magic was done, after careful collation and edition, from numerous Ancient Manuscripts in Hebrew, Latin, and French...　New Age/Occult Pages 92

☐ **Rubaiyat Of Omar Khayyam** *by Edward Fitzgerald*　ISBN:1-59462-332-5　**$13.95**
Edward Fitzgerald, whom the world has already learned, in spite of his own efforts to remain within the shadow of anonymity, to look upon as one of the rarest poets of the century, was born at Bredfield, in Suffolk, on the 31st of March, 1809. He was the third son of John Purcell...　Music Pages 172

☐ **Ancient Law** *by Henry Maine*　ISBN: 1-59462-128-4　**$29.95**
The chief object of the following pages is to indicate some of the earliest ideas of mankind, as they are reflected in Ancient Law, and to point out the relation of those ideas to modern thought.　Religiom/History Pages 452

☐ **Far-Away Stories** *by William J. Locke*　ISBN: 1-59462-129-2　**$19.45**
"Good wine needs no bush, but a collection of mixed vintages does. And this book is just such a collection. Some of the stories I do not want to remain buried for ever in the museum files of dead magazine-numbers an author's not unpardonable vanity..."　Fiction Pages 272

☐ **Life of David Crockett** *by David Crockett*　ISBN: 1-59462-250-7　**$27.45**
"Colonel David Crockett was one of the most remarkable men of the times in which he lived. Born in humble life, but gifted with a strong will, an indomitable courage, and unremitting perseverance...　Biographies/New Age Pages 424

☐ **Lip-Reading** *by Edward Nitchie*　ISBN: 1-59462-206-X　**$25.95**
Edward B. Nitchie, founder of the New York School for the Hard of Hearing, now the Nitchie School of Lip-Reading, Inc, wrote "LIP-READING Principles and Practice". The development and perfecting of this meritorious work on lip-reading was an undertaking...　How-to Pages 400

☐ **A Handbook of Suggestive Therapeutics, Applied Hypnotism, Psychic Science**　ISBN: 1-59462-214-0　**$24.95**
by Henry Munro　　Health/New Age/Health/Self-help Pages 376

☐ **A Doll's House: and Two Other Plays** *by Henrik Ibsen*　ISBN: 1-59462-112-8　**$19.95**
Henrik Ibsen created this classic when in revolutionary 1848 Rome. Introducing some striking concepts in playwriting for the realist genre, this play has been studied the world over.　Fiction/Classics/Plays 308

☐ **The Light of Asia** *by sir Edwin Arnold*　ISBN: 1-59462-204-3　**$13.95**
In this poetic masterpiece, Edwin Arnold describes the life and teachings of Buddha. The man who was to become known as Buddha to the world was born as Prince Gautama of India but he rejected the worldly riches and abandoned the reigns of power when...　Religion/History/Biographies Pages 170

☐ **The Complete Works of Guy de Maupassant** *by Guy de Maupassant*　ISBN: 1-59462-157-8　**$16.95**
"For days and days, nights and nights, I had dreamed of that first kiss which was to consecrate our engagement, and I knew not on what spot I should put my lips..."　Fiction/Classics Pages 240

☐ **The Art of Cross-Examination** *by Francis L. Wellman*　ISBN: 1-59462-309-0　**$26.95**
Written by a renowned trial lawyer, Wellman imparts his experience and uses case studies to explain how to use psychology to extract desired information through questioning.　How-to/Science/Reference Pages 408

☐ **Answered or Unanswered?** *by Louisa Vaughan*　ISBN: 1-59462-248-5　**$10.95**
Miracles of Faith in China　　Religion Pages 112

☐ **The Edinburgh Lectures on Mental Science (1909)** *by Thomas*　ISBN: 1-59462-008-3　**$11.95**
This book contains the substance of a course of lectures recently given by the writer in the Queen Street Hall, Edinburgh. Its purpose is to indicate the Natural Principles governing the relation between Mental Action and Material Conditions...　New Age/Psychology Pages 148

☐ **Ayesha** *by H. Rider Haggard*　ISBN: 1-59462-301-5　**$24.95**
Verily and indeed it is the unexpected that happens! Probably if there was one person upon the earth from whom the Editor of this, and of a certain previous history, did not expect to hear again...　Classics Pages 380

☐ **Ayala's Angel** *by Anthony Trollope*　ISBN: 1-59462-352-X　**$29.95**
The two girls were both pretty, but Lucy who was twenty-one who supposed to be simple and comparatively unattractive, whereas Ayala was credited, as her Bombwhat romantic name might show, with poetic charm and a taste for romance. Ayala when her father died was nineteen...　Fiction Pages 484

☐ **The American Commonwealth** *by James Bryce*　ISBN: 1-59462-286-8　**$34.45**
An interpretation of American democratic political theory. It examines political mechanics and society from the perspective of Scotsman James Bryce　Politics Pages 572

☐ **Stories of the Pilgrims** *by Margaret P. Pumphrey*　ISBN: 1-59462-116-0　**$17.95**
This book explores pilgrims religious oppression in England as well as their escape to Holland and eventual crossing to America on the Mayflower, and their early days in New England...　History Pages 268

QTY

The Fasting Cure *by Sinclair Upton*   ISBN: *1-59462-222-1*   **$13.95**
In the Cosmopolitan Magazine for May, 1910, and in the Contemporary Review (London) for April, 1910, I published an article dealing with my experiences in fasting. I have written a great many magazine articles, but never one which attracted so much attention... New Age/Self Help/Health Pages 164

Hebrew Astrology *by Sepharial*   ISBN: *1-59462-308-2*   **$13.45**
In these days of advanced thinking it is a matter of common observation that we have left many of the old landmarks behind and that we are now pressing forward to greater heights and to a wider horizon than that which represented the mind-content of our progenitors...   Astrology Pages 144

Thought Vibration or The Law of Attraction in the Thought World   ISBN: *1-59462-127-6*   **$12.95**
by William Walker Atkinson   *Psychology/Religion Pages 144*

Optimism *by Helen Keller*   ISBN: *1-59462-108-X*   **$15.95**
Helen Keller was blind, deaf, and mute since 19 months old, yet famously learned how to overcome these handicaps, communicate with the world, and spread her lectures promoting optimism. An inspiring read for everyone...   Biographies/Inspirational Pages 84

Sara Crewe *by Frances Burnett*   ISBN: *1-59462-360-0*   **$9.45**
In the first place, Miss Minchin lived in London. Her home was a large, dull, tall one, in a large, dull square, where all the houses were alike, and all the sparrows were alike, and where all the door-knockers made the same heavy sound...   Childrens/Classic Pages 88

The Autobiography of Benjamin Franklin *by Benjamin Franklin*   ISBN: *1-59462-135-7*   **$24.95**
The Autobiography of Benjamin Franklin has probably been more extensively read than any other American historical work, and no other book of its kind has had such ups and downs of fortune. Franklin lived for many years in England, where he was agent...   Biographies/History Pages 332

Name	
Email	
Telephone	
Address	
City, State ZIP	

☐ **Credit Card**   ☐ **Check / Money Order**

Credit Card Number	
Expiration Date	
Signature	

Please Mail to: Book Jungle
PO Box 2226
Champaign, IL 61825
or Fax to: 630-214-0564

ORDERING INFORMATION
web*: www.bookjungle.com*
email*: sales@bookjungle.com*
fax*: 630-214-0564*
mail*: Book Jungle PO Box 2226 Champaign, IL 61825*
or PayPal *to sales@bookjungle.com*

Please contact us for bulk discounts

DIRECT-ORDER TERMS

20% Discount if You Order
Two or More Books
Free Domestic Shipping!
Accepted: Master Card, Visa,
Discover, American Express

www.ingramcontent.com/pod-product-compliance
Lightning Source LLC
Chambersburg PA
CBHW080908020726
47502CB00008B/2381